William Selwyn

Winfrid

Afterwards Called Boniface, A.D. 680-755. Waterloo, a Lay of Jubilee for June 18,

A.D. 1815

William Selwyn

Winfrid
Afterwards Called Boniface, A.D. 680-755. Waterloo, a Lay of Jubilee for June 18, A.D. 1815

ISBN/EAN: 9783337142407

Printed in Europe, USA, Canada, Australia, Japan

Cover: Foto ©Andreas Hilbeck / pixelio.de

More available books at **www.hansebooks.com**

WINFRID

AFTERWARDS CALLED

BONIFACE.

A.D. 680—755.

The better fortitude
Of patience, and heroick martyrdom,
Unsung.

Paradise Lost, IX. 31

BY

WILLIAM SELWYN,

CANON OF ELY CATHEDRAL.

Cambridge:
DEIGHTON, BELL AND CO.
LONDON: BELL AND DALDY.
A.D. 1865.

A DAY of gloom; first showers, then pouring rain;

A narrow boat, adown the turbid stream

That eats the crumbling banks of Upper Rhein,

By vapour and the whirling current borne,

From Basel; neither hill nor tower to break

The weary length; but ever and anon

Harsh gratings of the iron-plated keel

On shallows, hardly passing: till at eve

The glorious Sun brake out beneath the gloom,

And burnish'd the broad flood, and touch'd with gold

The minster towers and pinnacles of Speyer.

Such close of such a day was emblem meet
To image forth the shining of that light,
Which after centuries of heathen gloom
Brake out upon the realms of Germany.

'Twas in the early spring of England's faith,
When Heaven had heard the Roman Father's prayer,
That Angles might be Angels; lingering yet—
As when the lingering winter struggles long
With rising summer, and the April days
Are mingled storm and sunshine—idol-gods
Struggled for life, and falsehood warr'd with truth,
And faith went halting 'twixt the old and new;
The strong man strove to hold his palace still,
Not knowing that a stronger shook his walls.
Then did the SPIRIT come upon the heart
Of Winfrid, as in Devon's upland vales
He worshipt GOD in CHRIST; his earnest life
Number'd not fifteen summers; yet was he
Fill'd with the wisdom of the fear of GOD.

Deep in all heavenly lore, and Spirit-taught;
He from his childhood, in his father's house,
Oft visited by holy men of GOD
In circuit, scattering Gospel-seeds, had loved
Long at their feet to listen; till the tale
Of JESUS, virgin-born in Bethlehem,
And in the SPIRIT going forth to break
The power of Satan, and the bitter Cross,
The grave, the victory, to the listening child,
Felt rather than believed, had grown to be
A life and power within his rising soul.

Then, not content to listen only, he long'd
To preach with his own lips the word of life,
And deem'd that GOD had call'd him; but his sire,
Kind though he was, thwarted his eager wish,
(A post of honour mark'd he for his son)
And would have had him live a layman still,
And carry on the lineage of his house,
Made noble by the blood of Saxon kings.

Ah me! in evil hour did Roman priests
Forge those sad fetters of the celibate,
Freezing the life-blood of the man of GOD,
Forbidding evermore the godlike names
Of husband and of father; woe the day!
But Winfrid in his heart was consecrate,
And his resolve, like flame before the blast
That has not power to quench, still gather'd strength
From what opposed it; thus they stood apart,
Father and son, still loving, but diverse
Their aims and purposes; when lo! the sire
Brought by a sudden seizure nigh to death,
And lying sick and sleepless, blamed himself;
Call'd for his son, and granted all he ask'd,
And pray'd for blessings on him.

      Winfrid went,
Bidding his father and his kin farewell,
And sought the holy house of Exeter,
To strengthen his heart-knowledge, gain'd by ear,
And print heaven's message deeper in his soul,

By reading holy writ, Prophet and Law,

And fourfold Gospel; thence still onward moved

To Nutescelle, sheltering under Winton's see,

Where woodland Hants o'er narrow channel looks,

To the fair Isle; and there, noviciate past,

A brother in that holy brotherhood,

And dedicate to GOD by priestly vows,

He bore his part in all their prayers and works,

And lived angelic days, now rapt to Heaven

In solemn litanies and chants of praise,

And now descending to the lowly huts

Of peasant neighbours, where his gracious tongue

Dropt manna for their souls in weary times.

Thus, like fair planet, round her central lord

Circling her peaceful path, did Winfrid run,

Ten years and more, his flower and prime of life,

The course of love his LORD had mark'd for him;

And as he ran, still brightening; till at length

The burning and the shining light he bore,

Though in frail earthen vessel, put to flight

The darkness and the guilt of heathendom,

And all the region round was fill'd with CHRIST.

    Now far and wide o'er Christian England spake

A voice as of a trumpet, loud and clear,

'Go forth, and preach the Gospel : freely give

'What ye received so freely :'—Whose the voice ?

Not Ecgbert's, but GOD'S voice that spake by him.

Ecgbert, now priest in Ireland, English-born,

When smitten down by sickness,—smitten too

By those sharp pangs that punish wasted days,

And gifts misused—in bitterness of soul

Had pray'd, like Judah's king, for added years,

And vow'd them all to GOD ; prepared himself,

And choice of faithful comrades, forth to go

Where scarcely yet the sacred name was named,

To forests wild, and wilder men that roam'd

Between the waters of the Rhein and Meuse,

In Friesland, cradle of the Anglian race.

    But while they girt themselves, and gather'd all,

The sacred books and priestly vestments rich.

Paten and chalice: troubled dreams by night

Foreshadow'd ill; their chief beheld the ship

Driven from her destined course by stormy winds,

Stranded and broken by the waves; yet still,—

Remembering how the great Apostle thrice

Had suffer'd shipwreck,—nothing terrified,

The little band moved cheerily to the port,

Where their bark lay for them, and went aboard.

But ere they sail'd, while waiting for the dawn,

A clearer vision came on Egbert's sleep,

And in the stillness of the night there fell

A voice of power from Heaven: 'This enterprise

'Is not for thee; return thou, and build up

'The desolations of thy land; the man

' By me for this work chosen I will send.'

He heard, obedient to that heavenly voice;

Went back to his own land, and labour'd well

To root out every plant of evil growth,

That marr'd the good seed of the Son of Man:

Yet not the less did Ecgbert sound the call
To Christian hearts in England, forth to send
The word of life to those dark pagan lands,
Rejoicing that some better man than he
Was chosen for that holy enterprise:
This was the trumpet-voice that moved the land.

Now for that mission-work beyond the seas
The leader call'd by GOD was Willibrord,
Long known in England's Church for fervent zeal;
He heard the call, and gladly gave himself
To plant the Cross in Friesland; forth he went
With chosen band, who loved not their own lives;
And Winfrid, still in Nutescelle, heard the call
Deep in his inmost soul; and though his kin
Strove, like the kin of Roman Regulus
Returning to his dread captivity,
To bar his way, he held his purpose firm,
And pray'd them not to fight against GOD's will;
And while he reason'd, Apostolic words
Rose to his lips unbidden; 'Woe is me

'If I preach not the Gospel.' 'Yea!' said they,
'Preach here in England; here are still enow
'Of Pagans, though they name the name of CHRIST :'
But he still answer'd calmly, 'Let me go;
'For I have heard a voice you cannot hear,
'And I have seen a hand, that beckons me
'To those far lands, now dark as England once,
'To help to make them light, as England now.'
　　So, seeing that his mind was fully bent,
They ceased, and Winfrid went to Willibrord.

And now what need to tell the Mission-tale?
How after tossing long in troubled seas,
And conquering gloomy doubts by faith and prayer,
They landed on the Frisian coast, so low,
'Twas almost lower than the wave they left :
And how through many a strange vicissitude,
Sometimes with kindness meeting, then with scorn,
And oft with blank indifference; sorely tried
By want of all things, and again made rich

Beyond their wants by hospitable hands;

They plied their Master's work, and sow'd his seed

Beside all waters; how they gather'd flocks

Redeem'd by grace from Satan unto GOD,

In all the villages and haunts of men,

In the wild forest, by the river's bank:

How men cast down the idols of the land

With their own hands that made them; and gave up

Their temples, timber-fashion'd, rudely carved,

To be the sanctuaries of GOD in CHRIST:

'Tis written in the life of Willibrord.

But there was none of all that holy band

So faithful or so wise as Winfrid; none

More ripe in counsel, none more bold in act,

None mightier in the Scriptures; for the lore

That he had learnt by hearing, or by books,

In his own land, in cloister, or at home,

Shone like a lamp to guide his daily life.

Scant time was now for reading; but the word

Of CHRIST dwelt in him richly; his the voice

To cheer faint hearts in peril or in woe;

In every time of trial came the chief

To take fresh counsel with his minister,

'For Winfrid's eye can see, though all be dark.'

And thus, when heavenly truth had won her way,

And Friesland was half Christian, thickly sown

With rising Churches, loath was Willibrord

To part with such companion of his cares;

And will'd that Winfrid should abide there still,

Bishop of Utrecht; gently warning him

That years and labours had impair'd his strength;

The good fight fought, he now should take his rest,

Pass quiet days of prayer among his flock,

Enjoy some foretaste of the promised bliss,

And leave to younger men the realms beyond.

But Winfrid had no heart to build his nest,

And take his ease, while all the Upper Rhein

Lay dark and fill'd with idols; onward still,

Urged by the native spirit of his race,

And by the fear of CHRIST, he long'd to press,

As debtor to the heathen of the South.
He answer'd firmly, 'Father, let me go;
'My GOD hath still a work for me to do,
'Ere the night come, when man can work no more;
'Labour to me is rest, and weakness strength;
'And I shall be more fruitful in mine age.'

But ere he launch'd on that tempestuous sea
Of heathendom, by sad example known
So full of peril to frail Christian bark;
He sought brief rest in his own native land,
And pray'd his friends in England to besiege
The throne of Heaven with supplications strong;
And chiefly Daniel, Winton's bishop, loved
And reverenced as a father. Then he went
To ask a blessing from that Mother-Church,
From whence a century since had issued forth
The mission of Augustine, which had tamed
Hard Saxon necks to the mild yoke of CHRIST,
In all the realms of England's Heptarchy;

To Rome he went; and with kind words of cheer,
The holy Father blest him for his work.

Then Winfrid, having braced his soul by prayer,
Amid the shrines of martyrs and of saints;—
Above his head Saint Peter's holy roof,
Beneath his feet the silent catacombs;
His heart with holy zeal and courage fill'd,—
Turn'd to his mission-field, and carried with him
A chosen band, like-minded with himself:
For his strong spirit, with mysterious power,
Magnetic, drew like spirits after him,
Where'er his orbit touch'd them.
                                    One he found
Whose name shall never in oblivion sleep,
While the Rhein rolls, and Friesland stems the sea:
One, fresh in youth and pure of heart he found,
To be the sharer of his coming toils,
Train'd for him unawares by Addula,
Abbess of holy sisterhood by Trier,
On Mosel's bank. There resting for the night,

In the refectory, at even-tide,
Young Gregory stood to read the holy page;
'And kenst thou what thou readest?' Winfrid said;
'Yea!' said the youth, and read the page again;
'Nay,' said the Father, 'that I question'd not,'
'Kenst thou the spirit of the holy word?
'Give me the meaning in thy mother tongue.'
   The youth was silent, for he could no more;
His heart as yet had found no utterance:
Then the good man, to all the sisterhood,
Pour'd forth, from the good treasure of his heart,
The spirit and the life that lay within
The letter of the Scripture; 'twas the word
Of JESUS in the porch of Solomon,
'And other sheep I have, not of this fold;'
'Them also must I bring, to hear my voice;'
Then spake he of the unbounded love of CHRIST,
And of the wild Thuringians, waiting still
For some to lead them to the Shepherd's fold;
The listening heart of Gregory caught the flame,

And ere he slept he begg'd of Addula
To send him forth as one of Winfrid's band;
'Had she no horse to give him?' then on foot
Would he accompany that holy man.

The Abbess was his father's sister; long
And lovingly she strove to bend his will;
Then yielded him to GOD, and sent him forth,
With horse, and all the best her house could give.

So these went forth and labour'd for the LORD,
Among the scatter'd flocks of Christians, few
And far between; and in the heathen wilds,
Where Thor and Woden, and the lights that rule
The day and night, usurp'd the place of GOD,
Maker of all things: which the harder task,
To quicken slumb'ring Christians, and awake
To his first love the Pastor's heart grown cold;
Or plant the Gospel fresh in wildwood hearts
Of Pagans, who shall tell? His varied work
Still Winfrid plied, as GOD ordain'd it for him.

To win, or to recover; and his band
Of faithful comrades, full of love and zeal,
Went forth to conquer further fields for CHRIST,
In ever-widening circles; year by year
Back roll'd the gloomy cloud of heathendom,
That brooded o'er the land; and churches rose,
And the fair temple of the Living GOD,
Built on the rock of JESUS crucified.

Four years had Winfrid labour'd thus, and saw
The harvest ripening round him; and the fame
Of idols overthrown, and multitudes
Confessing CHRIST their Saviour, came to Rome;
Thither too Winfrid sent his messengers,
With letters of good tidings, and besought
The Roman Father's counsel; but he said,
'Let my son Winfrid come himself to Rome:'
He rightly deem'd such work, so blest of GOD,
Should now be crown'd with higher dignity;
And Winfrid should return with fuller power,

As Bishop, to confirm and stablish well

The Churches of his planting. Winfrid came,

And slept not till his tale of joy was told;

Then after full confession of the faith,

And frequent interchange of holy thoughts,

And lastly, oath of firm fidelity,

Sworn on the shrine, where rests (so Rome believes)

The great Apostle, founder of their Church;

The Holy Father with a solemn choir

Of Bishops, laid his hand on Winfrid's head;

Nor rested there, but with unwonted speed,

(So dear the man, so paramount his work)

Thrusting aside the waves of other cares,

That daily surge from all the world on Rome,

Hasted to send him forth; yea! the next day,

Gave him the canons, written fair and large,

With letters to the Mayor of the Franks,

Martel, and other princes; charging them

To forward Winfrid's work with ready help.

　　Then once again he blest him, and ordain'd

That Winfrid should henceforth be Boniface,
By that name to be known throughout the world;
But Winfrid loved the name his father gave him,
And his own band of faithful followers
Would call him Winfrid still; for by that name
They knew him when their hearts were knit to his.

Once more their feet are on the Alps; once more
Their eyes are bent toward those Rhein-water'd fields,
Where they have walk'd with CHRIST, and yet would walk.
Right glad the welcome that awaited them
From all their faithful flocks, and from the sheep
During their travels added to the fold;
And glad the voice of Winfrid, speaking now
From the full heart of Christian Father's love;
His word went forth with power; and many a realm
Was added to CHRIST'S kingdom; and the Vine
Of the LORD'S planting stretch'd her boughs abroad,
From the great River far into the heart
Of Europe, 'twixt the Alps and Northern Sea.

ONE tract alone remain'd, untrodden yet
By any foot of Gospel-messenger;
The forest-tract of Geismar; far within,
Where never woodman's axe was heard to ring,
Mid streams and swamps, and trunks of ages past,
That lay along the ground where they had fall'n,
Moss-grown, and matted o'er with trailing plants;
And in the open glades, where daylight shone
At intervals, amid surrounding gloom,
Like joyful moments in a life of pain;
There did the Saxon idols hold their sway
Unchallenged; and the Christian people said,
Here was the strongest hold of Satan's power;
The very citadel of heathendom;
Could once the Gospel of the Living GOD
Pierce that dark forest, and disperse the gloom;
Then the whole land would soon be fill'd with light.

And Winfrid in his heart resolved to go,
Strong in the promise of the risen LORD,

'Lo! I am with you alway;' and he went,
With chosen followers, to the dreadful wood.

KING of that forest reign'd a giant tree,
An oak, beneath whose spreading shade might rest
An hundred horsemen, picqueting their steeds;
Five centuries, and more, of summer suns
And winter rains had knotted all his stem;
Uncounted moons, crescent and full, had gleam'd
Among the branches, chequering shade with light,
As the leaves trembled to the midnight air;
There had he thriven, overshadowing all,
Dwarfing all other stems that ventured near;
Till left alone in solitary state,
With ample space of verdant glade around.
And nought to intercept his majesty:
This tree was sacred to the Thunderer, Thor,
And well-nigh worshipt as the god himself.
No lack of vigour yet, for year by year
His wealth of leaves from every arm and branch

Pour'd freshly forth; but careful eye might mark
High on the topmost crown some naked twigs;
And one who stood beneath, close by the bole,
Might see a deep-cut trench, all weather-stain'd,
Cleaving the centre, widening to the bark,
With split and jagged edges: and they said,
This was the Thunderer's mark; for none but oaks,
Or seldom, were so scathed; and never yet
Did the great god with second thunderbolt
Strike the same tree; such was the heathens' tale.

And Winfrid's eye had mark'd that trenching cleft,
Not counting it for proof of sanctity,
But of GOD's might; so waiting for the day,
When Priests and Chieftains, and the common folk
By thousands, all assembled round the tree,
To dance in honour of the Thunderer Thor,
With horrid sacrifice and revelry;
Then Winfrid came, and standing in the midst
Like him who stood on Carmel for the LORD,
He cried aloud, 'Ye Priests and People, hear:

'How long will ye thus worship senseless trees?

'And sacrifice to them that are no gods?

'Lo! here we stand this day for life or death;

'Now call ye on your god; while I and mine

'Try with our axes this divinity:

'And if your Thunderer can avenge his own,

'Then let his lightning smite us; but if not,

'And if this tree fall down and split asunder,

'Then may ye learn that Thor is no true God;

'And bow your hearts to Him who made this tree,

'The Sun, the Moon, and all the host of Heaven,

'Our FATHER! and his CHRIST, the Tree of Life,

'Whose leaves are for the healing of the world.

    'Lo! here we stand this day for life or death.

'Will ye abide this trial?'   And they said,

'We will abide this trial.'

                Then the Saint

With axe in hand, and eyes upraised to Heaven,

Pray'd to the Living GOD, and struck a blow

Which cleft the bark; a second downward fell.

Meeting the first, and left a gaping notch;

Which two stout deacons with alternate stroke,

Deepen'd and widen'd, till the mighty trunk

Half round was sever'd; while the priests amazed

Look'd on with horror, calling on their god

To hurl his lightnings and avenge his own.

Five hundred rings and more, ring within ring,

Lie open to the centre, and the sap,

The giant's life-blood, trickles down the roots;

And yet no lightning falls, no thunder-peal

Speaks for the god; while Winfrid calmly stands,

Watching the end in holy confidence.

Slowly and sadly, and with many a groan,

The growth of ages yielded; till at length

A sudden blast bore down with perilous weight

On the broad leafy mass, and made the tree

Nod to his fall: then Winfrid with his axe

Sever'd the bark that girt the further side,

As yet unwounded; heavier still the wind

Bore down; and, like the ship unballasted,

That falls upon her side before the gale,
With one long crash the giant monarch fell,
And falling split, with fourfold havoc riven,
Ev'n where the lightning-bolt had cleft the stem.
 And with that fall the Thunderer's empire fell,
The baseless fabric vanish'd like a mist,
Before the rising Sun of Righteousness:
They cried 'the GOD of Winfrid, He is GOD:'
And from the timbers of the fallen oak
They built a House of Prayer to GOD in CHRIST.

 Thus did the last stronghold of Satan yield;
The last dark cloud of Error past away;
And all the land was fill'd with light and love.
Fair was the time, and Winfrid's heart was glad;
And through the forest-glades the merry noise
Of cheerful toil resounded; and the plough
Furrow'd the virgin-soil, and Christian hands,
Like Isaac in the land of promise, sow'd
The kindly seed, and reap'd an hundred-fold.

Praising the LORD of harvest.

Simple hearts,

Content to labour while they preach'd the word,

Were Winfrid's helpers, fitted well to win

The hearts of Hessians, rugged as their oaks.

But few were they to feed the growing flock,

And Winfrid wrote to England; 'Pray for us,

'And have compassion on your brethren here,

'Our Saxon neighbours; for they often ask,

'"Why do not more of England's teachers come

'"(Since GOD hath made us of one blood with them)

'"Over to us, and help us?" O my friends,

'The time is short; the night is drawing nigh,

'Help us, while yet 'tis day.'   Thus Winfrid urged

The mitred heads of England; not in vain;

His company of preachers multiplied,

And youthful scholars fill'd his cloister-walls,

Ripening for future service; women too,

Forsaking home and kindred, cross'd the sea,

Planted themselves in Christian sisterhoods,

E

And going forth on angel-ministries,
To feed the hungry, cool the fever'd lip,
To cheer the widow and the fatherless,
Taught pagan hearts to feel the love of CHRIST.

And soon the choicest of the Saxon youth,
Baptized, and train'd in Winfrid's school, began
To bear the Gospel-message to their kin ;
And elder heathen, hearing these discourse
Of the meek Saviour, and his life of love,
Half-won to CHRIST, but still reluctant, cried ;
'Ay! now the tree of our old faith must fall,
'For see! the branches sever'd from the stem
'Make handles for the axe that hews it down.'
Fair was the time, and Winfrid's heart was glad.

BUT lo! a storm-cloud, dark and terrible,
From the far East came rolling, with the sound
Of clashing arms, and empires overthrown;
O'er Syria's plains, and Persia's ancient realm,
O'er Afric's coast, and the green vale of Nile,

Swept like a mighty tide the Saracen host,

And made all Moslem; lands, where erst the faith,

Planted by Paul, water'd by Cyprian's blood,

Had flourish'd ; where Augustine pour'd the stream

Of living waters ; heard the evening cry

Of 'Allah and his Prophet.'   Then the wave,

With rage unbated, o'er the narrow strait

Dashing on Spain, o'erwhelm'd the sunny land,

All save one little kingdom girt with rocks,

That held her faith and freedom.

                                        Bolder still

It climb'd the parting Pyrenean ridge,

Hung for a while, dark-threatening, on the steep,

Then burst with havoc and wild ruin down

On the fair Frankish realm, and spread dismay

Through all her borders to the banks of Rhein,

Where Winfrid's churches trembled at the sound.

But soon the voice of GOD throughout the land

Awoke to arms the Christian chivalry ;

Karl Martel, with the banner of the Cross,

Fronted the Crescent on the field of Tours;
Received their fiery onsets all unmoved,
Six livelong days; then with the rising sun
For Christendom he charged, and laid in dust
Proud Abdalrahman, with his myriad slain;
Check'd that wild Eastern wave, and roll'd it back.

Then had the Christians rest, and multiplied;
And every man in peace and quietness
Sate under his own vine, and sang glad hymns
To GOD'S Eternal SON; on every side
Fair steeples shone, with sound of matin-bells;
And deep in many a shelter'd valley rose
The lowly kloster, with a school for youth;
And kindly cheer for way-worn travellers;
And healing for the sick; and holy words
Of peace and comfort for the broken heart.

BUT now on Winfrid's soul too heavily prest
The care of all the churches; and the time

Was fully come to parcel out the land
Won for the LORD, in meted bishoprics,
So lightening by division heavy toils:
Once more to Rome he went, and there received
Full power, as Legate for all Germany,
To found fresh Sees, and duly consecrate
Chief Pastors for the cities of the Rhein;
Each with his choir of elders counselling
The welfare of the churches clustering round;
Himself, as Primate, watching over all.

   Then on his homeward way, through Lombardy,
Refresh'd awhile with hospitable cheer
In Luitprand's royal mansion; and his soul
Kindled anew by choral antiphons,
In Milan's Dome, where once Augustine stood,
Not Christian yet, but listening there, to prove
If Ambrose were indeed so eloquent,
As fame reported of him; day by day
He listen'd, till the clear persuading voice
Moved him against his will, and made him feel,

Not that the man was eloquent of tongue,

But how divine the SPIRIT speaking in him ;

His word of GOD and CHRIST how true, how good.

Now, past the Alps, and past Bavaria's plain,

With Passau's bishop, in his lonely see,

Where the great streams of Inn and Donau meet,

The Legate takes sweet counsel; and provides

That ample realm with four-fold pastorate ;

And Winilo, well pleased, to other hands

Resigns the church-crown'd hill of Freysingen,

And Regenspurg, by Donau's rapid flood ;

And the fair tract, where princely Salzburg looks

From her own circling hills, and shining lakes,

To the great Watzman's glacier-cloven peak,

High-towering o'er the beauteous König-see.

SWEET as cold waters to the thirsty soul,

Are tidings from loved kinsfolk far away,

With hopes of meeting; such was Winfrid's joy,

When, coming to his Rheinland home, he heard,

That Wunibald his kinsman, lately met
In Rome, now mindful of his plighted word,
Was on his way to Winfrid's mission-field.
And with him came his brother, Willibald,
Who, after pilgrimage to Palestine,
Long toilsome ways, and perils of the deep,
Would fain have rested in still cloister-life,
But Winfrid's strong entreaties drew him forth.

Together came the brothers, and to each
His work was given; to Wunibald, the charge
Of seven Thuringian churches, young in faith;
To Willibald, a frontier-post to hold,
At Eichstadt, in a wild and woody waste,
Where one poor church was all that spoke of CHRIST.

Nor doth Walpurga tarry long at home,
Their sister; gathering to herself a band
Of faithful women, zealous of all good,
She braves the sea to join the work of GOD:
And while the others find their tasks of love
At points diverse, far scatter'd through the land;

While Thecla makes her home in Kitzingen;
And Lioba, by Tuber's winding stream;
And Chunitrude on Salzburg's mountain-side;
Walpurga near her elder brother founds
A convent for her sisterhood, and tends
The weak ones in the fold of Wunibald.

   How chafed the heathen remnant in their woods!
To see these outposts of another faith,
From a far isle, uprising in the land,
And breaking all their ancient solitudes,
Which they had peopled with imagined sprites,
Fairies and elves;—while hunters of renown
Swore fiercely that the boar and wolf should roam,
As in their fathers' days, to make them sport.
But soon the gentle life, and holy ways,
Of these meek strangers, blessing all around,
Making glad light amid a world of gloom,
Won savage hearts to peace and confidence.

   NEVER had Winfrid's sun more brightly shone,

Than now when seated on his throne at Mainz,

Encircled by the kinsfolk whom he loved,

All working with one soul for love of CHRIST.

    Had then Gewillieb died? or left his See?

'Twas vacant by Gewillieb's deed of blood:

He, bishop as he was, had lured the foe,

Who slew his father in fair field of fight,

Down to an island in the frontier-stream

That parted either host; there holding parle,

With his own priestly hand had struck a blow

Piercing the heart; and for that treacherous stroke

His priestly functions ceased for evermore.

    Then Winfrid, who had deem'd Koloin should be

The Primate's centre, fix'd his see in Mainz:

And now the region wide, on either bank

Of the great River, was all portion'd out

In peaceful bishoprics; and Winfrid's cares

Were lighten'd by division; but he long'd,

Before his ministry on earth should end,

To make the body of his Church compact,

All fitly framed; so calling round his throne
A synod, Church- and States-men join'd, they took
Full counsel for the welfare of the land.

Thus having order'd all, the aged Saint
Seeing his labours blest, would often go
To his loved shrine, by Fulda's quiet stream,
Where Sturm—whom he had cherish'd from a child,
As his own son—with weary toil and search,
Through trackless forest, riding on his mule,
And guarding both himself and mule at night
With rough-built palisade, but more by prayer,
Had found a fair, well-water'd, fertile spot,
Safe from the rude assaults of Saxon hordes:
And, gladly hastening thither, Winfrid's hand
Traced out the ground-lines of a goodly Church.

There often, leaving all the city-cares
To his auxiliar Lull, he loved to rest
With holy Sturm, and bathe his spirit deep
In that clear crystal-stream that issues forth
From GOD'S throne and the LAMB'S; sweet days of prayer

And joyful praise for all the LORD had wrought

By his poor servant; and where'er he came

Men look'd with reverence on his hoary head ;

And his old age was as the autumnal tree

Touch'd by the evening sunbeam : there he hoped

To yield his soul to GOD, and lay his limbs

Beneath that rising aisle.

                But suddenly

There came a tale of woe from Lower Rhein,

That shook the heart of Winfrid. Since the death

Of Willibrord, whose years of patient toil

Had planted CHRIST throughout the Frisian realm,

No shepherd like himself, zealous and wise,

Had risen to tend his flock ; and faith grew faint,

And love wax'd cold ; and idols rose again,

From many a lurking-place and covert cell,

Up to the light of heaven ; and savage frays,

Pagan with Christian warring, rent the land,

Trampling the kindly harvests under foot,

And many an holy altar ran with blood.

Then Winfrid could not rest; he heard again
The voice that call'd, he saw the beckoning hand;
He brook'd it not, that the fair field of CHRIST,
Sown with his seed, should thus be trampled down :
He thought on those victorious days, when he
With Willibrord, had borne the Cross on high,
Triumphant o'er the gods of heathendom;
And as the horse, of old in warfare train'd,
If haply in his pasture-field he hear
The distant cannon-boom, or thunder-peal,
Again he smells the battle, and again
With head high-raised, and nostrils all on fire,
Pants for the charge; so Winfrid's spirit rose,
And he must go to Friesland.

                                    All in vain
Did Lull, with all his brethren, urge his years,
His failing strength, and his well-earn'd repose:
He still replied : 'What would ye have me do ?
' But go in faith where GOD is calling me,
' And mine own heart; for well I know, my son,

'The time of my departure draweth nigh;

'Have I not number'd threescore years and ten?

'A crown of glory waits me. But do thou

'Continue the good work by me begun;

'The Churches of Thuringia stablish well;

'Root out foul error from the field of GOD;

'Complete my church in Fulda; where these hands

'Laid the first stone, be there my resting-place,

'When GOD shall call me; see thou lay me there.

'And now, my son, make ready for my voyage,

'Lay all my books and parchments in the chest;

'Forget not Ambrose on the gain of death;

'And over them a lych-cloth, fair and large,

'To wrap my body for the last remove.'

They wept, but said no more; 'GOD'S will be done.

Was inly breathed by all the brotherhood,

Who knowing they should see his face no more,

Yet hopeful of his victories for CHRIST,

Brought down their aged Bishop to his boat.

HE watch'd the fast-receding towers of Mainz,
With prayers for blessings on the flock he left;
Then as they vanish'd, braced himself anew,
With prayers for blessings on his work to come;
Then swiftly by the downward current borne,
Past where the Mosel yields up life and name,
Lost in the greater majesty of Rhein;
Past many a mouldering fort of empire gone,
And many a rising town of later days;
And hills and islands waiting for renown;
And past the Roman walls of proud Koloin;
They landed on the level Frisian bank;
And where an affluent of the River made
Almost an island, with a sheltering wood,
They pitch'd their lowly tents, and worshipt GOD.
There, while the aged saint, with lifted hands
And eyes, the priests and deacons kneeling round,
Invoked the help of Heaven; forth from the wood
There came a little company of men,
Two women in the midst, and knelt with them;

The remnant of the flock, the faithful few
Among the faithless many; these had held
Their love for CHRIST; His Cross upon their brows,
And His good SPIRIT dwelling in their hearts,
Kept them still His, amid the flames of war
From the live embers of old heathendom
Bursting so fiercely; from their desolate homes
They fled for refuge to the silent shade,
Here in the utmost border of the land.

  Prayer ended, 'Winfrid!' sounded from each tongue;
They knew him, though the lines of care and toil
Had deeply trench'd his face, and his thin hair
Fell snow-white on his shoulders; here were some
Whose foreheads Winfrid's hand had seal'd to CHRIST;
All from his lips had heard the word of life;
Now after glad embrace they spread the board,
Brought forth the sacred chalice, and rejoiced
In that perpetual feast of peace and love,
The sweet communion of the LAMB of GOD.

Then with fresh zeal went forth the Saint, to war
Against the foul relapse to heathen rites,
The faithful Gregory ever by his side,
Their fiery tongues denouncing gods of wood:
In many a peopled mart he stood unmoved,
Though face to face with heathen multitudes,
Fearing GOD only.
    When they saw the Cross
Gleam on his banner, heard the well-known voice
Telling of CHRIST forsaken, shame and fear
Fell on them, and their earlier faith revived ;
They fell before him suppliant to the ground.

Then kindly, wisely, lifting up their hearts,
Lest sorrow overmuch should whelm them quite,
He told of Peter, how his bitter tears
Found grace with Him who came to save the lost ;
How JESUS proved his quick-reviving faith,
By threefold question, 'Simon, Jonas' son,
'Lovest thou me ? lovest thou more than these ?'
Then in the stern words of the Son of Man,

Heard in the Vision of the holy John;

'Remember whence ye fell; repent and do

'The works of your first love, which ye have left.'

They heard, and with glad hearts obey'd his voice,

Dash'd down their helpless idols to the dust,

And built fresh temples to the Living GOD.

Thus o'er the land the Cross went forth in might,

And all was peace; if idols yet remain'd,

Or idol-worshippers, they were not seen

In public haunts, nor ever rear'd their front

Where men were gather'd for affairs of state;

But lurk'd in dens and caverns, shunning light,

With nightly homage soothing fallen pride;

And left the CRUCIFIED to reign alone,

Beneath the sun-lit canopy of Heaven.

THEN seeing that the LORD had blest his work,

The Churches all at rest, and multiplying;

New converts daily made, the old reclaim'd;

Baptismal dews sprinkled on every brow;

A hope, subdued before, now touch'd again
The heart of Winfrid ; 'When my work is done.
'I yet may see my own, and end my days
'In Fulda's sacred precinct; there find rest.'
Yet ever bowing meekly to GOD's will,
'LORD! as thou wilt ;' nor had he wish to go,
While aught in Friesland yet remain'd undone.

'Twas now the joyous holy Easter-tide,
And on the day that saw the Saviour rise
Triumphant o'er the grave, a goodly band
Of youthful converts had been seal'd to CHRIST,
By water and the SPIRIT ; and the time
Was fix'd, when all should meet by Burda's stream,
A central spot, uniting East and West,
To ratify their vows, and there receive
Fresh measures of the SPIRIT. On that morn,
Fill'd with the sacred joy of Pentecost,
Before the Sun was up, the Bishop sate,
Surrounded by his faithful company,

Prepared to lay his hands on every head,

Sign of the FATHER'S love o'ershadowing them.

Now through the drifting clouds bright streaks of dawn

Proclaim'd the day at hand; when faint at first,

A rising murmur, as of waving trees

Moved by the morning wind, was heard afar;

They fondly deem'd that swelling sound might be

The cheerful voices of the new-baptized,

Marching in gladness to the river's bank,

Where Winfrid waited; but anon they saw

Strange glitterings of the Sun's first level beam

On sword and lance, on-moving; nearer now,

And unmistaken, came tumultuously

Voices of terror, fearful cries and yells,

A mingled roaring as of wildwood beasts,

Made furious by long fasting: 'twas the foe!

The foe they thought so scatter'd and so crush'd,

The heathen foe, who in his covert close

Had mutter'd vengeance, and had watch'd his time.

Then hastily rose to arms the faithful band,

Seizing what offer'd first ; but Winfrid cried,

'Peace! peace! my sons ; CHRIST is the Prince of Peace ;

'We may not fight with weapons of the world ;

'This is the will of GOD ; and let us meet it,

'As men who know the body may be kill'd,

'But the soul lives for ever. Sure am I,

'That this shall be no hindrance to the faith ;

'The blood of martyrs makes the good seed grow ;

'Have we not read how after Stephen's death

'The Gospel spread more widely? Let us wait.'

So, like those white-hair'd Roman Senators,

Awaiting the assault of furious Gauls,

But with a better hope, they calmly sate.

Let others tell the deed of blood : 'tis said,

That Winfrid, holding as a shield before him

The volume of the Gospel, turn'd aside

The first lance-thrust aim'd at his saintly breast ;

Pierced was the holy book, but not one line

Or letter of the sacred text was marr'd.

Swift flew the tidings through the land, and woke

To righteous fury every Christian heart ;

Forth went the fiery torch, and roused to arms

The faithful in all Friesland ; swift they came,

Mustering for war; and when the third day rose,

Appear'd a goodly host, all fired with love

For their good Pastor, with avenging zeal

For him and fifty more, so foully slain :

Then dashing with fierce onset on the foe,

In wine and wassail madly revelling,

And each with other quarrelling for spoil,

Reckless of ill,—the Christians routed them

With utter havoc, and recover'd all,

Save what blind heathen rage had quite destroy'd.

    Nor ever from that day of victory

Did the false idols raise their heads again

In Friesland ; for the remnant of that day

Yielded to CHRIST, fulfilling Winfrid's word,

That death should be no hindrance to the faith :

His dying finish'd what his life began.

AND where was Winfrid's resting-place? at first
In Utrecht's inmost shrine : the people will'd it,
It was his land of labour, first and last ;
There-laid they him with solemn obsequies.
But when his follower in the throne of Mainz
Heard the sad glorious tale of martyrdom,
And where his body lay, he quickly call'd
The Council of his Church; and with one voice
An embassy to Utrecht was decreed,
With letters, pleading that the man of GOD
Left his last charge, wherever he might fall,
To lay his limbs in Fulda's sacred aisle.

    Slowly and sadly was the plea allow'd,
Slowly and sadly was he borne away;
One journey more, with many a rest between,
Where his dead presence moved the hearts of all
Who look'd upon his bier; and one brief time
Of sojourn in his own cathedral Mainz ;
And Winfrid is at home in Fulda's aisle.

    And there, once more, assembled round him dead

Those who had loved him living; there was Lull,

The Primate, with the bishops of his realm,

From all the daughter-sees around, that own'd

Allegiance to the Mother-Church of Mainz :

From Wurms, and Bamberg, Erfurt, Buraburg,

And from the rival towers of proud Koloin ;

And from the Upper Rhein, whose evening sun

Touches with gold the pinnacles of Speyer :

And there was Gregory, faithful to the last ;

All join'd with Fulda's abbot, holy Sturm,

To sound the requiem o'er the Martyr's grave.

There in a vaulted shrine, beneath the floor—

No light of outer day, but what might seem

The far light of that day when all shall rise—

There with hope-hallow'd tears, and solemn strain

Of choral song, ' *O death, where is thy sting !*

' *O grave, where is thy victory?*' they laid

The hands that crown'd the Monarch of the West,

The feet that went about, publishing peace,

The lips that preach'd the Gospel to the poor,

The heart that beat with love to GOD and man.

There still the Martyr from his silent cell,

Though dead, yet speaketh; and his earnest faith

Stirs noble spirits to brave deeds for CHRIST:

Thence do his pithy words of sharp reproof

Sound forth to all the lands of Christendom,

For frequent warning; 'Golden priests of old

'Were wont to minister in wooden cups;

'Now, wooden priests in golden chalices:'

And still, as every rolling year brings round

The nones of June, his day of martyrdom,

High festival is kept for Boniface,

Apostle of the LORD in Germany.

SONNETS.

Sabbath Morning, by Duddon River.

AUGUST 26, A. D. 1849.

— ✦ —

O THAT the SPIRIT'S gracious power may come
  Like rushing wind into our hearts this day,
  And bear us up to Heaven, while we pray,
On wings of faith and love! for while we roam
Delighted 'neath the sky's o'er-arching dome,
  Amid the mountain-glens, the torrents' play,
  The waving woods, the banks with flow'rets gay;
Still something fails; we are not yet at home:

Great GOD! our Father, help us now to soar
  In spirit to Thyself; make us rejoice
In hope of glory unseen; that we the more
  May love the hand, our cup of joy that fills,
  Our hearts be stedfast as the lasting hills,
  Our praise unceasing as the River's voice.

Reflexions.

‧ ✦

UPON the bridge we bent o'er Duddon's stream,
    Our parting look; while brightly there did move,
    Or rest, the images of all above;
The rocks; the island, waving gold and green;
Pen-Janet, capt with firs; and faintly seen
    The far-off hills; one cloudlet, white as snow,
    Hung trembling o'er the fall that foam'd below;
All else was Heaven's clear blue, or golden gleam:

Oh! canst thou, Duddon, from thy tranquil breast
    Give back each lovely hue of earth and sky,
    And all in vain on us doth Glory shine!
    O may the gracious SPIRIT purify,
And calm our troubled souls to holy rest,
    And GOD trace there his lineaments divine.

Remembrance of
Thomas Kynaston Selwyn.

D. JULY 5, A.D. 1834.

—⎯•⎯—

HADST thou been with us, Brother! how thine heart
  Would have delighted in this mountain-stream ;
  For thou, while here on earth, didst nothing deem
So lovely as the Rivers : on the chart
Thine eye would track their windings, and apart
  From all companions oftimes wouldst thou go,
  Where the bright waters into Ocean flow,
And taste, if salt or fresh.   But where thou art,

What tongue can tell thy pleasures, pure and bright ?
  What heart could wish thee still to linger here ?
Hope whispers, near the fount of love and light,
  Thou drinkest of God's River, crystal-clear ;
And thou hast learnt, how peaceful and how free
'The Spirit mingles with Eternity !'

55

Near Wilha's Bridge, Duddon River.

AUGUST 28, A.D. 1849.

I MARK'D the River, when his stream was low,
   Scarce gliding o'er the weir that checks his march,
   And leaving a dark line on rock and arch;
And much I marvel'd that the lordly flow
Of Duddon such vicissitude should know:
   In silent grief I stood; as knowing well,
   The stream of human joy doth often tell
Of sad decrease, all unforeseen: when lo!

Forth from the waters, on the morning gale,
   Arose a gentle and soul-thrilling voice;
"The River of God's Love can never fail;
   "Full from his Throne the living water flows;
   "There wash thy guilt away, and there repose;
"There quench thy thirst, and let thy soul rejoice!"

The Night of Sorrow.

August 10–11, A. D. 1869.

—◆—

O STRANGE dark night! the weary watches through
    I moved between my brothers, to and fro;
    One deeply slumbering, worn with toil and woe,
And one who, never sleeping, faintly drew
His failing breath; yet with firm heart and true
    Confest his faith in CHRIST, the Risen Life;
    With smiles of comfort cheering his sad wife,
And blessing all: our love no more could do;

But we could feel a gracious Presence nigh,
    Turning our night to day; and with the spring
    Of morn we gather'd round the sacred bed,
    And on the Bread of Life together fed;
The Bishop spake, "O death, where is thy sting?"
The Judge, "O grave, where is thy victory?"

To Charles Jasper Selwyn.

My Brother! all this golden Autumn-tide
  We range our wonted fields; and see the wain
  Rolling in gladness with rich store of grain;
The troops of merry gleaners; far and wide
We gather all the changes that betide
  Kings and their peoples; spell the syllables
  That tell of yesterday beyond the Seas;
And Thou—with folded hands, art laid aside,

Dark, joyless, cold, and lifeless—Nay! not Thou!
  Nought but the frail out-wearied earthly shell,
That held thee once, is lying here below;
  While Thou, still living, beautiful and bright,
    With thy loved LORD, in bliss no tongue can tell
Reposing, waitest for the perfect Light.

Remembrance of
Charles Jasper Selwyn.

—◆—

I LIVE with spirits past to realms above,
  As with those here abiding: oft by night,
  When all the Heaven is hung with cressets bright,
I walk and commune with the souls I love;
And deem that still I see them live and move,
  Free from all touch of pain, or shade of ill,
  In glad obedience to their Father's will,
Like Stars that from their pathway never rove:

And long to be with them: but chief with thee,
  My Brother! later-born, but earlier ta'en,
Who manfully didst bear sharp agony;
  And dying didst not leave us all forlorn,
  Taking the Holy Cup at morning-dawn,
In stedfast hope to meet in Heaven again.

WATERLOO.

Cambridge:
PRINTED BY C. J. CLAY, M.A.
AT THE UNIVERSITY PRESS.

WATERLOO

A LAY OF JUBILEE

FOR

June 18,

A. D. 1815.

It was a day of Giants.

Wellington.

SECOND EDITION.

𝕮𝖆𝖒𝖇𝖗𝖎𝖉𝖌𝖊:

DEIGHTON, BELL AND CO.

LONDON: BELL AND DALDY.

A.D. 1865.

To those who fell in arms, that glorious day,
But falling help'd to win it; and to those
Who shared the triumph, now have gone to rest;
To him who sleeps beneath the golden Cross;
And to the few remaining, ere the last
Shall pass away from earth,—this thankful lay.

For brave deeds, held in memory, will revive
In after days, when peril calls them forth;
GOD give us lasting Peace; GOD save the QUEEN.

William Selwyn.
June 18, *A.D.* 1865.

HARK! 'tis the day of rest; the matin-bells
Are sounding forth from every village-tower
Glad notes of Peace on Earth, good will to men;
And in the vale, between two gentle heights,
A little onward from the forest edge,
The fields are standing thick with rising corn,
Rejoicing in the plenteous rain of heaven.

B

But other sights ere long will meet the eye,
And other sounds will drown the Sabbath-bells,
And mar the Sabbath quiet; and the hopes   10
Of harvest from those fertile fields must fail;
For here two mighty hosts are met, to try,
Within the compass of a summer's day,
The last great issues of a long-fought war.

    Where then are all the golden dreams of peace,
That smiled on Europe but a year ago?
All rudely shatter'd! while the council sate,
Meting out kingdoms, and arranging terms
Of treaty, that should bind the world to peace,
Curb the strong powers of earth, and guard the weak,   20
By the firm sanctions of the general league;
Upon the council-table, in their midst,
Fell, like a thunderbolt from cloudless sky,
The startling word 'Napoleon is in France'!
And all their counsels turn'd from Peace to War.

    Then fast and frequent came the posts, that told
Of his triumphal march; how Lyon rose

And welcomed him ; how strong battalions, sent

To bar his way, turn'd round and follow'd him ;

How Ney, who boasted he would bring him caged   30

To Paris, caught the madness of the hour,

And rode once more as Marshal by his side :

Thus with glad welcome moving through the land,

Without a battle, daily gathering force,

He wins the city, mounts the vacant throne,

An Emperor, with his army, once again.

Then, master of an hundred thousand men,

He claims his right to be received once more

Among the brotherhood of sovereign powers ;

Accepts the will of Europe as his law,   40

And promises an Empire bent on peace.

In vain ! short, stern, and hopeless was the word ;

All Europe holds him outlaw : his return

Is breach of compact, troubling the world's peace ;

If he will still have empire, he must hold

His empire by the sword; for Europe's will

Is bent on crushing all his power to harm.

Now half the land was fever'd with delight,
And dreams of glory; no remembrance now
Of Russia's snows, or Leipzig's bloody days;   50
But all is full of promise; 'one campaign
'Of glorious war will set our empire high
'Above the nations, as of old': forth goes
The call to town and hamlet, rousing swift
The warrior hearts that had begun to rest
In peace and quietness, but loved it not:
Now sword and lance were furbish'd for the war,
And forge and foundry travail'd day and night;
Old comrades of the battles far away
Embraced again, and talk'd of victories;   60
The charger neigh'd, to find himself once more
In line with old companions of the field;
The Guard, Napoleon's Guard,—who oft of yore,
Ere evening closed upon the doubtful field,
Had turn'd the tide of battle,—fill'd their ranks
With younger blood of France, and form'd again
A living rampart round their warrior Chief.

And here he stands among them, as of old,

Adored by all; his mighty presence felt

Through all their ranks, inspiring courage high;   70

His master-spirit proved by timely march

Of all his legions to the field of war,

Converging on one line from points diverse,

While his foes doubted where the blow would fall:

He stands, already crown'd with victory,

The Conqueror of Ligny's hard-fought day;

And high-exulting in his well-wrought plan,

As having thrown himself between his foes;

The Prussians, beaten and in full retreat;

The English, face to face, within his grasp.   80

    But one beside him boldly spoke a word,

To check that overweening confidence,

The boast of one that putteth harness on;

As having known, by many a battle-field,

How well the British fight, how hard they die;

"Your army, Sire, will have sharp work to-day;

" That infantry was never known to yield."

And worthy of such troops the British Chief;
Who loves stern War, but for the fruit of Peace;
Dear to his men, as Cæsar to his Tenth;
Proved in an hundred fights; his soldiers know
That he will lead them, as he ever did,
Wisely and well; nor spend their lives for nought;
But watch his time; and never fail to seize
The moment that leads on to Victory.

The field was one their Captain's eye had mark'd,
As fitted well to stop invading hosts,
And shield from harm the Belgian capital:
But had his army been the same, as when
Behind the triple Torres Vedras lines
He stood at bay, and baffled all assault,
Though great Massena led the leaguering host,
Until the wearied Marshal back retired;
Then pressing forward, on Vittoria's field
Smote them, and scatter'd; drove them o'er the hills,
And follow'd them to France; had all been here,
Who bore him forward on that conquering march,

Perchance not here, but on the frontier line,

He then had stood in arms, and met the foe

With the stern voice of thunder from his guns; 110

'Thus far—no further shall thy legions come.'

But time and war have thinn'd his veteran host;

Brave Craufurd sleeps upon the breach he won;

And many a soldier of that gallant band,

The Light Division, moulders far away

Beneath the tropic sun, beyond the seas,

Their places ill-supplied; and Wellington,

Compensating his loss by favouring ground,

Where screen'd from view his men may rest, and take

The hill's advantage of assaulting foes, 120

Has laid his plan, with Blucher's promised help,

To bide the brunt of war at Waterloo.

So stood the leaders, on that Sabbath morn,

Each with his army marshal'd for the fight;

Both train'd to war from youth, both tried in fire,

Through many a deadly conflict; both unharm'd;

One bent on Glory; one to Duty true.

Had then the Great Disposer mark'd this day
In his far-reaching counsels? Were these two
Born for each other? destined here to meet?
One year's revolving sun had seen the birth
Of either warrior; and with all his might
The one had striven to mar the other's work;
And yet, through all these years of changeful war,
Ne'er had they met in battle-field;—and now
One little mile is all that severs them;
And less will be that interval ere night.

Dark were the heavens that morn; and dark was earth;
The low dull clouds hung heavily o'er the land;
The labouring guns dragg'd through the sodden soil,
Like Pharaoh's chariots in the Red Sea deeps;
But as the day uprose, the Sun unseen
Dried the wet earth, and thinn'd the veil of gloom;
And either host were busied with their arms,
Which the night-damps had silenced; rolling drums,
And clear-voiced clarions sounding o'er the vale,
Gave and return'd the challenge of the day.

Then, from their ridge, the British and Allies
A goodly sight beheld ; along his lines,
And through his squadrons, eager for the strife,   150
Girt with a gallant band of warrior chiefs,
Companions of his early conquering days,
Rode the great Emperor, in the pomp of war :
Less gaily clad, less splendid than the rest,
But more observed and better known than all,
On his white charger, in his redingote :
Glad shouts of welcome hail'd him as he past,
Answering his word of cheer; and martial strains
Swell'd forth, 'mid banners blazon'd with renown,
And fired their courage to its highest flame.   160

But on the other side, behind the ridge,
Lies strength of war, without the pomp ; and now,
All unattended, save by two or three,
And fearless, as in England's hunting-field,
But his heart beating with the pulse of war,
And kindling for the strife, the British Chief

Rides down the slope, and through the covering wood;
Scans a brief while the enemy's line; prepares
To foil their onset; cheers his garrison
With such brief words as stir the soldier's blood;   170
Then, calm and stedfast, to his height again;
For he has given the post to faithful hearts,
And valiant hands, to hold it to the last;
'Macdonell will not leave it while he lives.'

    Scarce had he rein'd his steed, and raised his glass,
To see if ought were moving; when the slope
Opposing, where it fell toward Hougoumont,
Shew'd a dark column, capt with gleaming steel:
And as it nears the covert, front and flank
Break, like the jagged edges of a storm   180
In act to burst; a cloud of skirmishers
Spreads o'er the field; and hark! sharp rattling fire,
Assailants and defenders answering quick,
Gives presage of the conflict fierce and stern,
Which round and through that frontier-post shall rage
The livelong day; the battle is begun.

Long time the strife hangs doubtful; to and fro
The edge of battle wavers; neither gains,
While both are losing momently; at length,
Outnumber'd by their foes, still thronging thick,
The gallant keepers of the wood, the men
Of Hanover and Nassau, slow retire;
And through the open fields, beside the wood,
Fresh foes uncheck'd are swiftly pressing on.

But short the triumph; see! the fiery charge
Of British Guards, has forced the victors back
From their brief conquest; and the plunging fire
From Bull's van-posted battery, deadly shells
Scattering dismay around, have clear'd the fields;
And all within the limits is regain'd.

Once more assaulting forces storm the wood,
Urged onwards by fresh columns from behind,
Still pressing forward, though the galling fire
Of Cleeves and Bolton gives them pause awhile;

These vex the front; while on the Western side
Another troop steals on, intent to find
Some opening undefended; once again
Before the thickening storm, from tree to tree,
Disputing every step, the Guards fall back:
The friendly hay-rick yields them breathing-space: 210
The orchard-trees give shelter, man by man;
And a brief respite stills the raging strife.

    Now, quickly following on the vantage gain'd,
The enemy deems the prize within his grasp;
'One fence to clear, and all will be our own;'
So thought they, and rush'd forward at the charge,
Leapt through the hedge—but here their course was stay'd:
No foe was seen; but sudden bolts of death
Laid low the leaders of their line; and those
Who follow'd saw before them, unawares,   220
A little fortress, wall and battlement,
And frequent loop-hole, rife with musketry:
And e'en the bravest quail'd before that sight;
Like men who bent on chase of flying deer,
Come suddenly on the lion in his den.

For Wellington, whose prescient eye foresaw,

That here the storm of war would earliest break,

Had counsel'd well to meet it ; all the night,

And all the morn, the busy hammers rang,

And plank and platform rear'd against the wall,   230

That wall too pierced, and crenellate above,

Made this the vantage-coign of all his line.

   While thus they stood dismay'd, and on their rear

Fresh masses still came thronging through the wood ;

Once more the roaring howitzers launch'd forth

Death-dealing shells among them ; and once more

The light and nimble guardsmen darted forth,—

Young soldiers running in that perilous game,

As late they ran in English cricket-field—

And well-nigh won the wood ; but like the men   240

Who see their harvests threaten'd by the sea,

And strive in vain to check the swelling tide,

Again they yield to numbers ; flying not,

But fighting backwards, selling ground for life :

At last, their sheltering hay-rick all in flames,

The enemy pressing round them, swift they rush
To the great gate that fronts the British height,
And entering, shut, and bar it as they can,
With all that offers readiest on the spot.

In vain; the dam is burst; the wave breaks in;   250
The foe has won his entrance; now the fight
That raged so long without, flames fierce within;
From every covert pours the deadly fire
From hands that know no yielding; and again
The Guards are rushing forth to open fight;
They struggle for the mastery, hand to hand;
Last, by main strength of arm, and firm resolve,
Five men, of differing rank, but one in heart,
Macdonell, Wyndham, Harvey, Graham, Gooch,
Force back the gate, and stem the rushing tide,   260
And close it in their face;—and those within,
The gallant leaders of the desperate strife,
Pay quickly for their daring with their lives.

Let Woodford tell what follow'd; he was there;
And he still lives; how, baffled thus, the foe

With daring onset, mid high-standing corn,

Vex'd man and horse of Smith's artillery;

While others, stealing on the Eastern side,

And joining those who press'd the orchard-front,

Drove Saltoun and his Guards from tree to tree;   270

And how the watchful eye of Wellington

Met each fresh move with fresh and swift defence;

How Woodford with his Coldstream fiercely charged

And broke the bold assailants on the right,

And threw himself within the fortress lines:

While Saltoun, strengthen'd, clear'd his ground once more,

The Scottish Guardsmen sweeping all the left.

Thus two long hours of mortal conflict pass;

And still Macdonell bides in Hougoumont.

WHILE thus the fight burns furious in the vale,   280

Above, on either ridge, flash sudden gleams;

The flame of battle runs along the lines;

And quick-replying thunders vex the air,

Till scarce an interval of rest remains;

And all below is wrapt in rolling clouds.

And now with higher aim, and heavier force,

The Prince of Moskwa, bravest of the brave,

Prepares to pierce the centre of the line,

And seize the road. Count d'Erlon, tried of old

In many a field of Italy and Spain,

With more than myriad host of infantry,

With half the steel-clad horse of Kellermann,

Advances to the ridge that parts the vale;

And in his front, commanding half the line

Of Wellington, his dread artillery.

NEY stood prepared, and waited for the word

From his great leader's lips; but ere that word

Was spoken, there appear'd a little cloud,

Like a man's hand, far off, upon the right:

Napoleon saw, and look'd again; and bade

His marshals and his staff scan warily

That cloud mysterious; some declared 'twas nought,

But trees; while others deem'd it, troops on march;

Soult said, ''tis Grouchy joining on our flank';

One, keen of eye, beside Napoleon, cried:

' I see the Prussian colours'; then the face

Of the great Emperor grew pale as death;

As if the ghost of injured Josephine

Had come, as Julia came on Pompey's sleep,

Embittering war's reverse by cutting words;

' With thy first love thy strength is gone from thee.'

    That cloud is destined, like the Pillar-cloud,

A light to Israel, dark to Egypt's host,

To turn the balance of the doubtful day;

'Tis Bulow, foremost of the Prussian march;

And Wellington now deems him near at hand,

And cheers his line for struggles soon to come.

    Time presses now; the morning hours are lost;

These English must be crush'd ere Blucher come;

The word is given; and o'er the ridge are seen

The heads of d'Erlon's columns; down they move
In serried masses, shouting for the strife;
While o'er their heads the deadly thunderbolts,
Swift messengers of doom, prepare their way.

'Aye' said the British Chief 'this is the game
' He loves to play; he thinks to make a chasm
' Right in our centre with his hundred guns,
' And then to plant his forces in the chasm;
' Well! let him try; it shall not serve him here;
' He shall find hearts that care not for his guns.'   330
So bidding all keep close behind the crest,
He let the roaring cannon speed their bolts,
Above his ranks, all harmless to the rear:
Save where a wavering line stands full in range,
Upon the outward slope—why posted there,
Right in the hottest of the battle's front,
Let others tell, I know not.—On they come;
The vale is past; they mount the hill, like clouds
That sweep the mountain-side with moving shade;

Four columns strong and deep: one leftward bends   340
Across the road, and laps round Haye la Sainte,
Where Baring and his German Legion true
Hold fearless watch and ward; the other three
Move forward, throwing forth their skirmishers,
And either front glows warm with answering fire.

Early that morn, while spying out his foes,
And measuring strength with strength, Napoleon ask'd,
'*Where are the troops of Picton?*'—Near the road,
Commanding all the centre of the slope,
The post of peril, and of glory, his,   350
By right of never-yielding hardihood.
Full on his front the central columns move;
The roaring thunders of the cannon cease;
The drums are beating for the charge; and loud,
And louder still the shouts of onset come;
For now they near the crest. Here Picton's eye
Was watching every step; he held his men
All eager for the onset; few were they

Against so many; relics of the day,

The glorious deadly day of Quatre-Bras,   360

When d'Erlon's men march'd to and fro, unscathed;

Thin was his line, two deep, with no reserve

To help in time of peril; fearful odds

It seem'd, three thousand to thirteen; but well

He knew their steadfast hearts; and as the foe

Appear'd above the ridge, he brought them up,

Three fighting regiments of Kempt's brigade,

And with sharp volley smiting the first ranks,

Ere they could open for a wider front,

He gave the word to charge! and through the hedge   370

They burst with a loud cheer, and forming quick

Their broken line, with level'd bayonets,

On rushing with the speed of sudden death,

They pierced the stagger'd column, broke its strength,

And bore it backward down the slope again.

　　But that proud sight their leader never saw,

For while he cheer'd them on with voice and hand,

His word of onset ringing in their ears,

Above the din of strife; a deadly bolt

Pierced that bold forehead, fronting to the foe;　　　380

He reel'd upon his horse—but ere he fell,

Brave Tyler, ever at his leader's side,

Lifted him down, and laid beneath a tree;

Then rush'd to battle to avenge his fall.

MEANWHILE the leftward troops of d'Erlon's line

Are pressing Haye la Sainte; and Baring's men,

Outnumber'd, slow retire to sheltering walls;

Till strengthen'd by the men of Luneburg,

Sent timely to their aid by Wellington,

They sally forth, to win the ground they lost:　　　390

Brief hope! fresh foes are close upon their front,

The upward-charging horse of Kellermann;

Ere they can form, or flee to safer ground,

The swift-pursuing cloud of cavalry

Has caught, and crush'd, or scatter'd all their ranks,

And captive droops the flag of Luneburg;

The remnant join the little garrison,

Within the leaguer'd walls of Haye la Sainte.

BUT when the Chief of England's cavalry,

The gallant Uxbridge, saw on d'Erlon's left   400

The steel-clad horsemen form'd in proud array ;

And all the vale as far as Papelotte,

Fill'd with his moving mass of infantry ;

His soul was fired ; for now, in open field,—

Far better than when yester-eve he turn'd

On those who strove to harass his retreat,

Across the narrow bridge of strait Genappe—

The French should feel his prowess.

                  Swift he sped

To noble Somerset, and Ponsonby,

And summon'd all their squadrons to the charge ;   410

And he, to rouse their spirit to full height,

Joining the Household line of Somerset,

Rode foremost of front rank, and shared with them

The peril and the glory of the day.

    Then as the enemy's horsemen clear'd the ridge,

All dazzling in their panoply of steel,

And thought to dash upon the British squares,

As they had crush'd the men of Luneburg;

He raised his sword, and gave the welcome word;

The clear-voiced trumpets spoke along the line,   420

And all rush'd forward like the rolling wave.

　　Dire was the shock of those two meeting lines,

As when two ocean-tides at highest flood

Meet in mid-channel; horse was wedged with horse,

Man clash'd with man: a thousand burnish'd blades

Gleam'd high in air, again descending swift

In strokes that cleft the limb, and reft the life;

And wounded chargers, freed from riders' weight,

Rear'd, plunged, and stagger'd in that troubled sea.

　　How shall they part? awhile right gallantly   430

The Eagles brave the Lion; banners cross

In waving tumult; and emblazon'd there

The victories of old, "Peninsula,"

"Marengo," "Friedland," meet amid the fray;

At length, o'erpower'd, the steel-clad warriors yield;

Unwilling trumpets sound the quick retreat;

And all have vanish'd o'er the ridge again.

BUT on the left of Somerset's brigade,
The deep-sunk track of Wavre broke the charge
On either side; and down the shelving banks,   440
And through the hollow way, the Cuirassiers,
All hotly follow'd by Life-Guardsmen, fled
In race tumultuous; till they cross'd the road,
(Just where the Rifles held their sandy knoll,)
And mingled with the fray, where Picton's men
With conquering shouts came charging down the hill.

But there they rein'd their steeds, and turn'd and fought,
Each man with his pursuer, hand to hand;
There valorous deeds were done in single fight,
Recalling ancient days of chivalry;   450
Still the Life-Guardsmen tell around their fires,
How Shaw with his own sword nine warriors slew;
And how, unharm'd by any foeman's blade,
He fell at last by carbine's deadly aim.

Now further still to left, brave Ponsonby

Stood ready; his brigade not vainly named

The UNION, for three kingdoms here were met;

The English Royals, with the Scottish Greys,

And Irish Inniskillings : in his front

Were Alix and Marcognet, mounting fast

With shouts of triumph ; but between the lines

Pack's Highlanders stood waiting for the foe :

While, anxious well to time his line's advance,

Close by the hedge in front watch'd Ponsonby,

And at the favouring moment waved his plume ;

Then in strong Union charged the Kingdoms Three.

Scarce had the Highlanders, at shortest range,

Return'd Marcognet's fire ; with level'd steel

Ripe for the charge ; when thundering in their rear

Came the Scots Greys ; and opening quick their files.

As best they might, they gave the horsemen way ;

But some who brook'd not such delay, nor loved

To see the battle won by other hands,

E

Held on their stirrups as they trotted through,

And with them fell upon the startled mass ;

'Scotland for ever!' was their battle-cry ;

With Scotland's pibroch sounding in the midst :

Short strife was there ; the downward-rushing wave

Whelm'd in its bosom, as it swept along,

The close-pent column ; dashing some to earth, 480

Some hurrying forward, powerless to strike,

Till all the ranks were rent with wild turmoil.

Full in the centre of that heaving sea,

Gleam'd bright the Eagle of the Forty-fifth ;

' Invincibles,' men named them ; never yet

Had they been foil'd in battle ; on the folds

That waved beneath shone many a storied name,

Wagram, and Eylau, Jena, Austerlitz ;

Girt with a sacred band it moved on high,

The oriflamme of fight. Brave Ewart saw, 49?

And in his heart resolved ; and dashing on,

By strength of arm and skill of hand he won,

And back to Bruxelles bore the glittering prize.

On! Gallant Greys! Napoleon marks your work,

And sternly praises with a warrior's joy:

'*See how they travail*'; but he threatens ill;

On! terrible Greys! but not too far!

They leave

The Highlanders to gather to the rear

The captives, all disarm'd; then downward still

In wild career, as rolls the avalanche,   500

Mix'd with the flying crowd they rush, and fall

Full on Marcognet's column of support,

And crush his last battalions, like the first.

The troops of Alix, mounting o'er the ridge,

With joyous shouts, like men who win a post,

Met England's Royals, charging up the slope;

(The rightmost of the line of Ponsonby)

Then all their shouts were still'd; they had not thought

To meet with horsemen there; no time had they

To give the greeting fit for cavalry;   510

They threw a scattering fire, then turn'd and fled

Back to the ridge ; but ere they reach'd the fence,

Meeting their rear still pressing forwards, heard

And felt the trampling of too swift pursuit,

And roll'd in tumult helpless down the hill.

    An Eagle shône amid that flying crowd,

Gift of Napoleon's Austrian bride ; a guard

Form'd hastily round ; but ere they could attain

The shelter of their succouring column, Clark

Right-shouldering forward with his squadron, smote   520

The standard-bearer to the death ; and saw

The standard fall upon his charger's neck :

' O break it not,' cried Stiles, who caught the flag,

And gave it to his Captain ; 'break it not';

For Clark was fain to thrust the golden bird,

For safety, in his breast : so all entire,

Eagle and colour, to the rear were borne,

To cheer the fainting hopes of Belgian hearts.

    Where is that succouring column ? downward borne

By their own flying comrades, and the weight   530

Of England's charge, and broken with dismay

By fresh disasters seen upon their right,
They rush disorder'd to the valley's foot.

For close upon their right, few minutes since,
The central squadrons of the Union line,
The Inniskillings, fired with rivalry
Of Scots and English, conquering left and right,
Came downward charging, with their wild Hurrah!
And at their fullest speed, with crushing weight,
On the rear right of Alix fiercely fell.   540
    Then Erin had her hour, and cleft and drove
The yielding mass; but where it yielded, spared:
And as the reaper lifts the beaten corn
That droops to earth, and fills his arm with sheaves;
The victors reap, unharm'd, their fallen foes,
And sweep a goodly harvest to the rear.

    Thus did one hour behold the proud advance,
The wreck, of d'Erlon's columns; not for lack
Of valour, but of skill and leadership:

Strong for assault, but helpless to resist;
Without one troop of horse to guard their march;
A ready prey for daring cavalry.

Now all 'twixt Papelotte and Haye la Sainte
Was fill'd with wild confusion; horse and foot
Mingled together; combats hand to hand;
Battalions bending to the furious storm;
Shouts for the mastery; cries of vanquish'd men
Asking for life; War's revel raging high:
And here and there amid the battle-wreck,
The horses that had lost the guiding hand
Champ'd the green corn, unmindful of the din;
But, when fresh troops came charging, form'd in line,
And rush'd with empty saddles to the fray;
While others, weary of their wounded life,
Convulsive paw'd the ground, and strove to die.

Oh! had the conquerors known their time to hold,
And spare their panting steeds! but on they sweep
In mad career, all heedless of the cries

Of captains, and the rallying trumpet-call :
Brave Uxbridge looks around for his supports ;   570
But they have swept far onwards.

                              At the foot
Of that destructive ridge, with cannon crown'd,—
Where the road piercing made a hollow way,
Choked with the flying mass—the Cuirassiers
Turn'd round on their pursuers, face to face,
And each man fought his foe ; till from the hill
Sharp musketry drove back the British horse :
One only, 'twas the Duke's own regiment,
The Royal Blues, had kept their order'd line ;
On their close squadrons rallying, Somerset   580
Drew back his horsemen from that wild pursuit.

But on the left, straight up the enemy's hill,
Rode a mix'd multitude of both brigades ;
The King's Dragoons, the Second Life, the Greys,
Royals and Inniskillings ; on they press ;
They crown the ridge ; and wheeling sharp to left,

Dash on the guns that raked the British line,
And spare not man, nor horse.

                    Too daring feat!
Too quickly doom'd to vengeance: now are seen
The pennons of French Lancers bearing down;
Fresh, strong, and well-array'd: no hope was then,
But in swift flight; and none could swiftly fly;
For every horse was spent, and the soft ground
Of the soak'd fields betray'd each foundering step.

    Full half their strength the Union lost that hour:
There fell, to rise no more, brave Hamilton,
Commander of the Greys; far o'er the ridge
Men said they saw him last: and Fuller fell,
Leading the King's Dragoons; and he, the Chief,
Who in his breast Rose, Shamrock, Thistle, bore,
Chief of that threefold Union, Ponsonby;
Well-proved in Spanish fields, and loved of all;
In vain he strove to check that wild career:
In vain his charger strove to save his lord,
'Mid the deep furrows of a new-plough'd field;

His last thoughts turning to his wife and home,
Pierced with lance-thrusts, he breathed his soul away.

And worse had been the issue of that hour,
And few had lived ; but in their sorest need,
His help too long delay'd by hindering ground,
Full on the Lancers' flank came Vandeleur:
His Twelfth—the Prince's plume and Rising Sun—
Pierced the last column of Marcognet's foot ;
Then with their comrades of the Light Sixteenth,
In one strong line they roll'd the Lancers down,
And saved the remnant of the daring Greys.

No time nor truce was then for either host
To tend their wounded, or remove their dead :
'Tis said, that some who lay upon the field,
Sore smitten, but yet living—say no more !
Let such things be forgotten, but good deeds
Of Chivalry and mercy never die :
One lived to tell, the younger Ponsonby,
How wounded in both arms, the sword and rein

Dropt from his palsied hands; how borne away
By his ungovern'd charger up the hill.
All helpless on that fatal ridge he fell;
And while he lay and bled, a kindly hand,
Foeman, but friend in time of need, applied
The life-restoring cordial to his lips,
And placed a pillow for his drooping head.

Now sad at heart the Marshal cross'd the vale;
And sad at heart, behind the sheltering ridge,
Count d'Erlon gather'd up his shatter'd force;
And told his loss; by thousands swept away;
By thousands dead, or dying; captains lost;
Lost eagles; guns disabled; ruin'd hopes.

BUT on th' opposing ridge, a goodly sight
Was seen by either host; for Wellington,
Girt with a gallant band of warrior-chiefs,
Companions of his early glorious fights,
Princes and ministers of Powers allied,

Rides forth with joy, and lifts his plume on high,

To greet brave Uxbridge and his horsemen home:

Loud shouts of glad acclaim rent all the air,

Far sounding o'er the vale; heart-stirring cheers,

Cheers for the Household, for the Union cheers;

Yet nought so moved the British Chivalry,

As that brief word from their great Captain's lips,

With the right hand of welcome to their Chief,

UXBRIDGE, WELL DONE!

BUT Tyler turn'd aside

From all that band of living conquerors,

From all the greetings of that joyous hour,

And sought, with two loved comrades of his chief,

The sad still spot, where PICTON, calm in death,

Alone with glory, lay beneath his tree.

Then were they first aware he bore a wound,

Of two days since, a livid galling wound,

Untended save by rude appliances;

36

Which, had his soul been made of stuff less stern,   660
Might well have stay'd him from this second field.

All sudden and unlook'd for to his men
Came that death-stroke; but not to him who died;
His heart had long foreseen it. When the call
To join his ancient leader drew him forth,
(For he had promised that in time of need
His arm should not be wanting) leaving home,
When near the borders of his native Wales,
He, passing by a church and open grave,
Leapt suddenly in, and measuring with his length   670
That narrow cell, said 'Such a place as this
'Will soon be all that I shall want on earth.'

His men will still rush on, and evermore
Remember him, when battle rages fierce;
And deem they hear his rough but cheering voice,
'Come on! brave ragged rascals.' He is fall'n;
Fall'n—but to rise again in after wars,
In many a soldier from the hills of Wales;
Who knowing how he lived, and how he died,
Will gladly yield up life for victory.   680

How fares the while the long-vext garrison

In Hougoumont? Still sorely vext; for still

Both Foy and Jerome pour their thousands down;

Some raining bullets on the fortress-wall,

Some venturing fresh assault on either flank,

Still meeting swift repulse;—and every hour

Fresh companies of guardsmen from the ridge

Recruit the thinn'd defenders;—few return :

The living stream flows down from either hill,

Then sinks ingulf'd in earth. Brave Saltoun's Guards

Have dwindled to an handful; yet with these

All undismay'd he holds the hollow way

Behind his orchard; till relieved at last,

From three long hours of instant watch and toil,

By Hepburn's fresh battalion. Then once more,

With one strong rush the orchard is their own,

E'en to the southern-bounding hedge.

                                   And now

Napoleon, chafing under long delays,

Large forces wasted in the bootless strife,

Bids plunging fire-balls wrap the place in flame,   700

The deadliest foe of all. What tongue can tell

The horrors of that hour, where none might move,

From his allotted post, to help and save

The helpless wounded from the raging fire!

    ' Oh! for that Power which saved the Hebrew youths

' In the red furnace'! Mercy heard the cry;

While some, unmurmuring, clasp'd their hands in prayer,

And passed away like martyrs to their crown;

Some fell asleep, unconscious painless sleep,

'Mid dreams of rushing waters; others saw   710

Within the little chapel, where they lay,

The flames just entering kiss the SAVIOUR'S feet,

And there, uncheck'd by mortal hand, die down.

    BUT not the raging flame, or stifling heat,

Avail to quell that steadfast garrison;

Though all within, and all around their walls

Is fill'd with death; the living guard their dead.

None knows one moment whether life or death
The next shall bring; for life or death they stand,
Each on himself relying, as if all
The battle rested on his single arm.

Thus two hours more of deadly conflict pass,
And still Macdonell bides in Hougoumont.

Now with fresh fury charged the cannons roar
From either height; the oldest warriors said,
Never did such continuous thunder-peals
Shake heaven and earth: and now with truer aim
That iron storm sweeps o'er the British ridge,
Rending the patient ranks that lie behind:
While shells infernal, bursting in their fall,
'Mid the down-lying columns havoc spread;
Or plunging in soft earth, break forth again,
Like the long-pent volcano, scattering death.
'Good practice that,' said Wellington, unmoved,
When the round shot came crashing through his elm,

'They did not use to fire so well in Spain.'

He saw his faithful Fitzroy Somerset
Reft of right arm, while watching by his side;
He saw his friend of youth, De Lancey bold,
Hurl'd by the rushing of a cannon-shot
Sheer o'er his horse's head, and dash'd to earth
Prone on his face, rebounding where he fell;
Brave Gordon pray'd him not to venture thus
His precious life—the life of all his host—
Then fell beside him, smitten with death-wound:
And all around him, staff and orderly,
Have felt the storm; swift death, or stricken limb,
Or steed disabled, thin the gallant band;
His own brave chestnut, at the rushing whiz,
So sharp and shrill, uneasy paws the ground;
And *'let us part a little,'* he cries, *'we make*
' Too good a mark for their artillery.'

Then oft the Chief would move along his lines,
And speak awhile with officers and men,

In homely phrase ; '*Hard pounding, gentlemen,*

'*But who will pound the longest?*' and when some

Pointing to weak battalions, shook the head,

And question'd of retiring ; '*Never fear!*'

He calmly said, '*We'll win this battle yet:*'

And when brave hearts, that could not bear to see   760

Their ranks all idly wasting under fire,

As melts the snow-drift smitten by the sun,

Pray'd him to lead them on ; '*Not yet, my lads,*

'*A little while, and you shall have your turn.*'

Once too when word was brought him, that the guns,

Near on his right, were level'd on the spot,

Where stood Napoleon planning fresh assault ;

Quick, stern, he answer'd, '*No! I'll none of that;*

'*'Tis not the work of leaders in the field*

'*To fire upon each other; tell him, No!*'   770

WHY do the thunders of the cannon cease?

—The awful calm that goes before the storm—

For now the gallant cavalry of France,

G

In all their glory, helm and cuirass bright,

Are moving to the front; and bugles ring

Sharp notes that stir the blood of man and horse

To deeds of daring; down the slope they pour

In proud array, and fill the vale below:

There rides Count Milhaud, with his Cuirassiers,

Bright steel on breast, dark horse-hair plume above; 780

Then, light and swift, Lefebvre-Desnouette,

Red Lancers of the Guard, with fluttering flags,

Chasseurs Imperial, dight with green and gold;

Twice twenty squadrons, in three glorious lines;

And with them Ney, the bravest of the brave:

Till all the fields where waving corn had been,

Between the eastern road and Hougoumont,

Are waving now with pennon and with crest,

On-rolling like the ocean waves. And lo!

Bright flashes sudden gleam along the ridge, 790

Mid wreathing smoke, and the quick-following peal;

And o'er their heads the death-bolts speed their way

To that opposing line, where now the word

Runs through the ranks 'Prepare for cavalry!'

So fierce that iron hail, so searching true

The range, that they who felt it long'd to see

Their enemy on the hill; and all too slow

Seem'd his brief passage o'er the vale between;

For as the minutes sped, each with it bore

Some brave ones from their post, and rents were made,   800

And fast and frequent came the cry—'Close up.'

'*Poor Cooke! he's gone!*' so mourn'd the Grenadiers;

A ball rebounding struck his shoulder-blade,

And hurl'd him from his square, and cast him down;

But one of hopeful heart, who loved him well,

Allix, his brother captain, went to see,

And found him stunn'd, but living; raised him up,

Set him on horse, and sent him from the field,

Safe from the trampling hoofs, which else had soon

Crush'd out, and quench'd, the feeble spark of life.   810

Welcome the crests and pennons on the hill!

Welcome the gleam of sabre and of lance!

That iron hail hath ceased. Now opening quick
Each square gives passage to the cannoniers,
Flying in haste before the surging wave,
Ere yet its breaking whelm them; there awhile
Within the hollow of each bristling square,
Or crouching 'neath the foremost bayonets,
They take their welcome refuge, and are safe.

For every square was like a castle-keep,   820
With banners floating proud and confident,
And warders watching for the coming foe,
And living walls for stone; within those walls
The Leader throws himself, and cheers his men,
By his own cheerful looks, and kindly words;
'*Now, Ninety-fifth, stand fast! We wont be beat;*
'*What would they say in England?*'—'*Fear not, Sir,*
'*We know our duty.*' And he feels secure,
As if within deep-moated fortress-walls.

But those who watch'd that upward charge, and heard   830
Their tramp, like far-off thunder, fondly deem'd

That nought could stand before them; now they win

The cannon, that made havoc in their ranks

Advancing up the hill; now rushing on

To greater glory, on those living walls,

And through the intervals of square and square,

Pour, fierce and fearless as the billowy sea,

The cavalry of France; with swelling tide

Surrounding and concealing all the rocks

That split their squadrons; yet those rocks stand fast,   840

Those waves no inlet find; but evermore,

As on they rush, their currents turn aside;

So fixt those living walls, so terrible

Those fronts of steel, out-breathing wounds and death.

    Then all along the bridge of war were seen

Riders unhorsed and horses riderless;

And 'mid the fitful peals of musketry

Was heard the charger's shrill and tremulous voice,

Calling his lost companions of the fight,

And scared with his own freedom from the rein.   850

    Meanwhile Napoleon chafed—'Why bide they thus?

'Surrounded so, and press'd on every side,
'Their guns all taken, their position won,
'By all the rules of war they ought to yield,
'Lost is the battle.'

But they knew it not;
One only rule they knew; there fast to stand,
And hold the ground against whatever came,
Until their leader gave the word to move.

And there they stood, or knelt, and look'd the foe
Full in the face as often as he charged,   860
Like men who meant to win the fight at last.

Once more the trumpet sounds to charge! but now
The ground is thick with dead and dying steeds;
Their path lies over dead and dying men;
Their squadrons intermingled hopelessly;
Weaker and wearier every fresh assault;
And as they pass beyond the chequer'd squares,
In dim disorder, Uxbridge sounds the charge!
And forward rushing in their bright array

British and German squadrons sweep the field,   870
And drive the many-tangled multitude,
Yet here and there resisting to the death,
And send them swiftly o'er the ridge again.

Then rose from every square a thrilling cheer;
And joyous greetings pass'd from man to man;
To see the host, that came with swelling flood,
Like the spent wave retreating. Then the squares
Open'd again, and forth the gunners rush'd,
And launch'd their bolts upon the flying foe.

But one there was who scorn'd inglorious flight,   880
Nor let those iron thunderbolts pursue
The warriors of his leading: near the guns
He rein'd his charger, waved his sword on high,
And threaten'd death to all who ventured near;
There a brief space, enough to save his men,
Enough to win the crown for rescued life
Of others, by the offering of his own,

He held his post; then died a soldier's death,
Wearing his crown, and honour'd by his foes:
Would that my lay were hallow'd by his name!

890

Again those gallant squadrons mount the ridge,
After brief respite in the vale below;
But warier now, one half assault the squares,
Half keep their order'd line; now once again
O'er all the death-strewn field the trial comes,
Of dashing valour match'd by patient strength,
The rolling breaker, and the steadfast rock:
Again the chequer'd squares throw back the waves,
Recoiling, raging, eddying to and fro,
In ever-mingling currents, brokenly.

900

Then oftimes would some fiery spirit rush
Alone and reckless on the bristling edge,
Tempting the face. to squander precious fire,
And make the charge a safer enterprise;
But all too wary for such wiles were they,
And kept their wrath until the squadrons came

Close on their front, full charging; then they gave
A volley such as made them reel away,
And broke their wave, and roll'd it right and left,
And strew'd the ground afresh with dying men.

Well stood the British, well the Germans stood ;
And the fresh youth of Brunswick, dark as night,
Beyond all praise, like veteran warriors stood ;
Avenging well their Duke's sad glorious fall,
Upon the hard-fought field of Quatre-Bras.
But while they stood thus firm, indissoluble,
Among them many a death-bolt found his mark ;
Far on the right, where from his lofty tower
The miller watch'd the fight, the Twenty-third,
The Fusiliers of Wales, had held their square
Impregnably; but near the close they saw
Brave Ellis, their commander, wave his hand,
To give him passage through the rearward face :
Thus, smitten in right breast, and faint with loss
Of life's fast-ebbing stream, he rode away,

Declining every proffer'd help, to die
Alone, or live, as Heaven should order for him;
He would not thin his ranks in danger's hour.

Five times did dauntless Ney renew the fight;
Napoleon gave him all his cavalry;   930
Guyot, with all his squadrons of the Guard,
And all the steel-clad corps of Kellermann,
Famed for the charge that turn'd Marengo's day,
The day of battle lost, and won again.
Once more the shout of triumph on the ridge,
The barren triumph of deserted guns;
Once more the daring charge, the sidelong swerve,
And all the wild careering round the squares;
Once more, the leaders prodigal of life:
Till wearied out at last with fruitless strife,   940
Thinn'd front and flank by ever-crossing fires,
Crush'd by the deadly aim of Bolton's guns,
Swept back by Somerset's and Dörnberg's charge,
Their spirit fails them, and they come no more.

WHILE thus the battle of the waves and rocks
For three long hours was raging on the height,
More and more hotly prest in Haye la Sainte
Brave Baring, with his German Legion true,
Still holds his own; still Carey, Græme, and Frank,
Each in his quarter, foil their thronging foes,   950
Repair the breaches, quench the raging flames,
Meeting each fresh assault with fresh device.

But hard the struggle; there no fortress-wall,
With battlement and platform fitted well;
Their workmen had been call'd away at night,
To arm the stronger fort of Hougoumont;
The very door, that closed their sheltering barn,
By wet and weary soldiers was consumed,
To feed the fire that warm'd their midnight meal;
But, worst of all, the soldier's life and strength,   960
The means of saving life by others' death,
Wasted and fail'd;—once—twice—and once again,
Did Baring send his urgent messengers;
Fresh succours came of men; but no supply

Of what his hungering rifles needed most:
None knew where lay the fault; but Wellington,
As ever, sparing others, not himself,
Took all the blame; '*I should have thought of that,*
'*But in the heat and hurry of the day*
'*I could not take in all.*'
                So foil'd at last,
Brave Baring with his remnant of brave men,
Wounded, but still resisting, leave the place,
And join the line. Now with exulting shouts
The foemen swarming seize the conquer'd post;
And what had been a strength, becomes henceforth
A thorn to vex the side of Wellington.

THOSE conquering shouts far sounding o'er the vale
Roused all the weary host round Hougoumont
To fresh and furious strife; again the fight
Within the orchard, wavering to and fro,
From hedge in front to hollow way behind;
But still the dauntless hearts of British Guards,

53

The loopholed walls, the guarded battlements,
Defied all comers, held the fortress safe.

And when the Prussian Baron, charged to keep
Unfailing intercourse between the camps
Of Wellington and Blucher, joins the Duke,
Where, near his tree, he scans the changeful field,
The Duke cries proudly, pointing with his glass,
'*You see, Macdonell still holds Hougoumont.*'

900

THUS all those hours, from noon till now the day
Was verging to its close, the battle raged
Unceasingly; and yet no sign appear'd
Of victory, or defeat, on either side:
It seem'd that Death, the common foe of all,
Should be the only Conqueror that day;
As if each host should sullenly hold at night
The post that each had held at morning's dawn;
And that the field that lay between should be
Like to that valley, which the Prophet saw
In vision by the bank of Chebar's stream,

1000

The dreadful open valley, fill'd with bones,
And there were very many, very dry.

  Brave Ney, so foil'd with all his cavalry,
Sent to Napoleon, pressing urgently,
For foot-battalions;—fretful was the Chief,
The day's disasters clouding o'er his brow,
New dangers hourly threatening on his flank;
' *Where would he have me find them? does he think*
' *That I can call up soldiers from the ground?*' 1010

  And oftimes while the long mid-summer day
Wore heavily on, and minutes seem'd like hours,
For greatness of the deeds that mark'd their flight,
For greatness of the issues hanging on them;
Oftimes the British Leader watch'd the hour,
And wish'd that Blucher, or the night, would come.
  And more than once there came a pressing call
For fresh supports to weak battalions, thinn'd
By that unceasing fire; but '*I have none,*'

He answer'd; '*he and I, and every man,*   1020

'*Must keep the ground we stand on, till we die.*'

   And when his dearest friend in battles ask'd,

'And should you fall, what orders would you leave ?'

'*Hold fast this ground, and bide in Hougoumont.*'

   And now, perchance, he wish'd a word might bring

Those fresh battalions in his time of need,

Which, posted far away for caution's sake,

Watch'd lest the foe should turn his right, and seize

The western road to Bruxelles; all the day

They held their post, and neither horseman came,   1030

Nor voice of cannon told them of the fight;

Though here ('tis said), in England, anxious ears

Caught faint and fitful, on the varying breeze,

The battle-thunder borne across the sea.

   AND where was Blucher? toiling on his way,

His weary way from Wavre; since the time

When first Napoleon spied that little cloud

Above Saint Lambert, he had labour'd on,

Through yielding sand, and through the strait defile,

Where confluent streams from hills on either side   1040

Had deepen'd all the tracks with mire and sludge.

Right manfully his gunners fought their way,

Winning each step by toil and strength of limb:

But more than once they cried in sheer despair,

'We can no further go—nor horse nor man

'Can bring our cannon through the pass'—but he,

Whose name was ever 'Forwards!' answer'd quick,

'We must, my lads, for I have pledged my word,

'To be with Wellington, ere day decline;

'You would not have me fail in time of need;   1050

'Another pull! and we are through the worst,

'And victory waits us—hark! the fight grows fierce!

'Once more! she moves again! now roll her on.'

Thus cheering all along the labouring line,

The noble veteran, reckless of himself,

Disdaining other carriage than his horse,

Forgetful of the rude and perilous fall,

That in the field of Ligny laid him low,

While the French cavalry went charging by,

Moves forward; till they win the Paris Wood,

Finding no foe to bar their entrance there;

Then wait, till all their elements of war

Shall gather into one dark brooding cloud.

But now he waits no longer; though but half

Of Bulow's force is there, half toiling still

Up the steep valley's side; he hears the guns

With long deep thunder storming all the line

Of Wellington; he sees the furious charge,

The oft-returning tide of cavalry;

A horseman comes fast-spurring from the Duke,

To press his speedy joining on the field;

While, far to left, dark looms Napoleon's Guard,

In serried columns, eager for the word

To strike the last great blow.

> '*Forwards!*' he cries;

And with his cannon opening on the line

Of Domont's horse, proclaims to friend and foe,

That he is come to take his part in fight.

I

Napoleon hears; he sees that cloud of fear
Darkening his east horizon; all his flank
Imperill'd by fresh foes; while Ney in front
Is pressing for supplies of infantry:
What infantry has he to spare for Ney?
Compell'd to succour Domont's yielding line,
He sends his last battalions, save the Guard,
To check the daring Prussians, ere they come
To mar his plan of battle.
                                    But too late!
Had Lobau timelier seized the Paris Wood,
While Blucher struggled through the deep defile
Of the rain-swollen Lasne,—far other then
Had been the turning of the scales of war.

Now all too late he comes; for Bulow's force
Completed, in strong columns issuing forth,
With all his guns and all his cavalry,
Moves down the slopes declining from the wood,
And forces gallant Lobau, overmatch'd,
Out-flank'd on right and left, but every step

Still fighting while retreating, Parthian-like,
Back to the road. And now across that road,
Hard by Napoleon's post, the Prussian balls
Are falling 'mid his last reserve, the Guard.   1100

Marr'd is his plan of battle, utterly ;
For he had thought to strike with all his Guard
Full on the weaken'd line of Wellington,
And sup in Bruxelles. 'When will Grouchy come ?
' Come soon he must, or Blucher's forward troops
' Will seize on Planchenoit, and molest our rear.'
But Grouchy comes not : and the younger Guard,
Eight strong battalions, led by brave Duhesme,
With thrice eight guns, must now prevent the foe,
And hold the village, till the day is won.   1110

MEANWHILE the Prince of Moskwa, doom'd to fight
With weary few, where many fresh have fail'd,
Combines the remnants of his infantry,
Gathers the fragments of his gallant horse,

For one more great assault. Not columns now—
Past loss has made him wiser—spreading clouds
Of skirmishers, with cavalry behind,
Shall harass all the line with galling fire.

From Haye la Sainte, their prize so hardly won,
They vex the Rifles on their sandy knoll,   1120
And force them back; then from their sheltering walls
In swarms out-spreading wide they sally forth,
And pour continuous hail on Alten's squares,
Indenting with sad gaps each forward face.
'*Form line!*' cried Alten to brave Ompteda,
Impatient of such unrequited loss;
Now Ompteda by long experience knew,
That curtain'd by that cloud of tirailleurs
Lay cavalry in wait; but when his Prince
Repeated in hot haste the rash command,   1130
Forthwith he broke his square, advanced in line,
Drove back the swarm before him;—and beheld
The ambush'd line of steel-clad cavalry
Dash quick as thought on his unguarded flank,

And crush them utterly; then fell himself,
A martyr to stern duty's high behest.

Now all along the line, from Papelotte
To where the ridge looks down on Hougoumont,
Fierce pours that broken but continuous storm;
Fiercest on Maitland's Guards, in square advanced,   1140
And Adam's Rifles; but the Leader's eye
Mark'd how they suffer'd more than they could harm;
He bade the Guards form line, and drive them down.
    'Tis done—the square re-form'd; the enemy's horse
Who thought to take them ere their ranks could close,
Met fire and steel, and shatter'd swerved away,
By Colborne roughly greeted as they past.

    AND now the end draws nigh; Napoleon deems
The Prussians check'd, his flank and rear secured;
Though fierce and furious still round Planchenoit church,   1150
Thrice taken and re-taken, burns the fight;
He bids his Guard prepare; right welcome came

That summons to brave souls, who all the day
Had watch'd inactive, while their comrades fought:
And when their Emperor cried '*All follow me!*'
Their valour kindled to its highest flame.

    Once more a dreadful lull; the guns are still;
The Guard is moving!—but athwart that calm
Of nearer thunders came the far-off roar
Deep-rolling of an hundred mouths of fire,   1160
On all their right, in answering cannonade.

    It troubled all their host; and most of all,
Napoleon; but to quell the rising dread
He sends his horsemen spurring through the field,
To spread the tidings wish'd for, but not true;
'*'Tis Grouchy joining battle with our foes.*'

    Then while fresh courage breathed from every heart,
And flash'd from every eye, he gallop'd down
On his white Persian to the forward ridge,
Commanding Haye la Sainte: there took his stand,   1170

And watch'd his Guard march past. They marvell'd much,

As each battalion came, to find him there ;

Had he not cried aloud, 'All follow me'?

And deep through all their ranks, to the last man,

Had sped the word, ' *The Emperor leads us on.*'

But there he stood, and pointed, as they past

In martial pride before him, to the height

That he would have them take, and win the way

For him to Bruxelles : there, not wholly screen'd

From harm, but shelter'd from the hottest fire,

He waved them on.

                Far other seen of old,

At Lodi's bridge, or when at Arcola

He dash'd through all the thickest storm of war,

A standard in his hand, and won the day ;

Their Leader then, now but their Emperor.

    Yet faithful how they march'd ! no faltering step,

No quailing brow was there ; but every man

Look'd his last look on him for whom they fought,

As though they sadly said, in passing by,

Like the doom'd swordsmen of the Flavian shows,   1190
' Thy Guard salute thee on their way to death.'

Oh! strange sad sight for Heaven and Earth! to see
These veteran warriors of an hundred fights,
Men of Marengo, men of Austerlitz,
Scar-furrow'd brows, and breasts with glory mark'd,
Compell'd to stake their laurels and their lives
On the frail chance of that last desperate throw!
    Yet frail it seem'd not, as they cross'd the vale,
With measured tread, two columns deep and strong;
With cavalry to rearward; on their flank   1200
Stern Drouot with his dread artillery;
And leader of the whole, with voice and sword
Breathing around his own unconquer'd hope,
Making the brave yet braver, dauntless NEY.

Now once again Napoleon's hundred guns
Blaze forth above his columns; and again
British and Germans bide the storm unmoved;

While Wellington with all his best reserves

Strengthens the shatter'd centre ; from the right

No longer prest by foes, he brings the men   1210

Of Holland and of Brunswick, yet unscathed;

And from the left, where Ziethen now has join'd

With welcome succour, come the light brigades

Of Vandeleur's and Vivian's cavalry.

    Still fresh were they ; they had not borne the brunt

Of wasting fight ; with dread surprise they view'd

The central havoc. *Where is your brigade?*

Cried Vivian, riding up to Somerset ;

' *Here!*' said he, pointing to two squadrons thin,

The remnant of the morning's two brigades ;   1220

Then to the field, where men and horses lay

In death, or hopeless life.

                 But now the ridge

Near Haye la Sainte, and every rising knoll,

Was cover'd all at once with musketeers,

And iron hail unceasing thinn'd the ranks

Of Kempt and Lambert; there in briefest space

                                          K

The Inniskillings-foot lost half their men:
Then, bolder still, forth from the covering walls
Field-guns roll'd o'er the hill, and grapes of death
Shatter'd the squares of gallant Kielmansegge;   1230
'Tis said, one face was wholly blown away,
And the brave men of Hanover closed in,
Three sides, where had been four; and all the while
The rolling drum-beat, sounding to the charge,
Proclaim'd the marching columns in their rear.

 Now came the time of peril; never yet
So trembling hung the balance; never yet
So nearly fail'd the centre of the line:
For now not with one arm alone they come,
But horse and foot combined, with galling fire   1240
Of musketry, and cannon at close range;
In vain did princely Orange lead the men
Of Nassau to the charge; they fail'd; the Prince
Was smitten to the shoulder-bone; and now
Brave Alten sorely wounded left the field;

Wounded was noble Halkett, who all day
Had cheer'd his men, and with them braved all deaths;
In vain the Brunswick columns hasten'd on
To fill the perilous gap; for there they met
A storm of balls, so fierce and merciless,—   1250
They stagger'd—and the foe was on their front,
In strong array, down-bearing—oh! if then
The Leader's eye had slumber'd, if his heart
Had quail'd before that onset,—who shall say?—
But Wellington spurr'd forward! hand and voice
And glance of fire roused every fainting soul,
And rallied all the line!

                But once again—
While Wellington rides off to right, to watch
The coming of the Guard—the daring swarm
Of skirmishers press on, and force the men   1260
Of Brunswick and of Nassau to the rear,
Till stopt by the close files of Vivian's Tenth—
—Hark! to the rolling drums! brave Kielmansegge
Is rushing to the charge, with Hanover,

And with the German Legion; Brunswick now
Fresh-couraged, and the men of Nassau, join
That forward rush ; brave Vivian cheers them on,
And gallant Shakespeare, all their cavalry
Strengthening the rear,—Hurrah ! the ridge is won,
The foe is falling back adown the slope ;   1270
British and German standards crown the height ;
The sorest peril of the day is past.

Now through the rolling clouds the Chief descries
The two strong columns marching o'er the vale,
While, on his left, unconquer'd d'Erlon still
Advances; and on right, round Hougoumont,
Fields, wood, and road, are swarming thick with foes,
For one more desperate strife. On come the Guard,
With shouts so loud and joyous, all men deem'd
Full surely that the Emperor led them on.   1280

It seem'd as if both columns, as they near'd
The British height, would join their confluent streams,

Making one torrent irresistible,

And bear down all before them.

                    But the first

Lay open to the forward batteries

Of all the right, which smote them flank and front,

And cleft their ranks, and laid their Generals low;

There Friant fell, sore smitten; Michel, slain;

And there was halting, for brief space; but quick

Reviving to de Morvan's thrilling cry,   1290

'*Forward! still forward!*' on they charge again:

The dauntless NEY, his horse kill'd under him,

Unsheathes his sword, and waves it o'er his head,

And leads the way on foot.

                    And now they rise

Above the ridge, and rising seem to grow

To more than human stature; but there meet

A fierce and deadly storm from Napier's guns,

Which drives their skirmishers, and breaks the head

Of their advancing column; yet advance

They must and will: and now, the ridge o'erpast,

Through the dim veil of smoke no force appears

To bar their onward march—when suddenly

Scarce fifty paces from their front arose,

Call'd up by one brief word from Wellington,

As from the bosom of the earth, a line

Of British Guards, four-deep, compact and strong;

And from that line pour'd forth such deadly sleet,

Three hundred fell at once, to rise no more;

Their front was shatter'd.

        All in vain did Ney

Cheer them to face that unrelenting storm;

They faced it, but it broke them, while they strove

To open wider front of answering fire;

Disorder grew each moment; some turn'd round,

Some fired at random—

        Then spake Wellington,

' *Charge! Maitland!*' then the gallant Saltoun cried,

' *Now's the time, boys!*' and with a thrilling cheer

Forward they rush, and drive the loosening mass,

Rent into fragments, o'er' the ridge again.

THOSE two strong columns had not join'd in one!
A brief, but fatal, distance sever'd them—
Twelve minutes—so the Guards who drove the first,
And follow'd them along their downward track,
Were ready for the second.
                              Ere they came
Undaunted by that deep discomfiture,
Maitland returning form'd his line afresh,
Oblique upon their right; while on their left
Deep-furrow'd, as they march'd, by Adam's guns,
The gallant Colborne wheel'd his regiment,
His Fifty-second, 'unsurpass'd in arms,
Since arms were borne,' to make them feel his fire,
Full on their long-extended flank; in front
They saw the mouths of Napier's battery.

Brave veterans! worthy of a better fate,
And wiser leaders; what could soldiers do?
So closely mass'd, so grasp'd in death's embrace?

They did what soldiers could; they plied their arms,
Each for himself; they struggled to deploy;
They faced on Colborne, gave him fire for fire;
But his strong line, four-deep, in firm array,
Full charging, with three hearty British cheers—   1340
The Rifles quickly joining on the left—
Quite broke their shatter'd ranks; and opening out
They cover'd all the slope in scattering flight:
And left upon the field, where they had stood,
Their column's form and measure sadly traced,
By dead and dying men.
        Then Wellington,
Defensive now no longer, gave the word,
And Adam charged still onwards; that repulse
Had turn'd the tide of battle; on they swept,
Driving before them all the mingled crowd,   1350
The flying Guard, and d'Erlon's fragments, struck
With sudden panic dread; for not alone
The Guard's repulse had spread dismay around,
But every stiller moment brought the roar

Of Blucher's cannon; and that false report,

Of Grouchy's succour, credited no more,

Now fill'd all hearts with deep despair and rage.

Still momently the panic terror spreads,

Like some mysterious current flashing through

The troops that press the British line; the fire   1360

Slackens; the swarm gives way; the tide is turn'd;

And with one mighty backward-streaming ebb,

Like the great wave that drags the beach away,

The hosts of France recoil.

                    But Wellington—

Who saw across the vale some squadrons still,

The remnants of the morning's cavalry,

In order'd · files—with Uxbridge counsel takes ;

And soon the line of Vivian's light brigade,

Cheer'd loudly, as they pass, by Vandeleur's,

Is charging down the slope, to strike at once   1370

Full on that last reserve, ere yet the Guard

                            * L

Can rally from their overthrow; ere yet
Ney or Napoleon can recover strength,
Or rouse brave spirits to fresh enterprise.

BUT when the Emperor saw his faithful Guard
So broken in that first assault, he cried
'*They are mingled all together!*' yet with speed
He rallied all the remnants that escaped
From Maitland's charge;—but looking once again,
He saw his second column, like his first,   1380
Stopt in their course, pursued along the slope;
And Adam's bayonets in bold advance
Down-bearing on his post—his face grew pale
As death; he shook his head for grief, and said;
'*All over now! 'tis time to save ourselves.*'
   Yet once again his soldier-spirit spake;
'*Better to die upon the field!*' but Soult
Laid hand upon his rein, and led him off
Within strong square of his own Veteran Guard.

THE BRITISH CHIEF survey'd with eagle-eye

The sudden change that swept across the field;

The mingled throng of his retreating foes,

The proud advance of Adam's strong brigade,

And Vivian's charge, where Robert Manners rode,

A horseman train'd in Belvoir's hunting-field,

Cheering his gallant Tenth, in nobler chase;

He saw, and felt that now his time was come,

To seize his tide of battle at the flood,

And ride upon the crest to Victory:

He gave the word to all his line, "ADVANCE."

And when some friend, more cautious, faintly urged,

'Our line is weak, the enemy still is strong;

'Were it not better that we wait awhile,

'Till in full force the Prussians succour us?'

'*No!*' said the Chief '*we've waited long enough!*'

''*Tis now my turn; let every man ADVANCE!*'

He saw that their defence was gone from them,

Their guard defeated, they would fight no more;

The Prussian guns were thundering on their flank,

Nearer and nearer still; the British right   1410
Had curved upon their left; the wall of fire
Was closing round them; 'twas the time to strike.

THEN all who lived arose, and mann'd the ridge,
All forward pressing as the foe retired;
The Chief himself stood high, and waved his plume;
High floated all his banners, battle-rent;
Loud peal'd the voice of trumpet, and of drum;
And clear and joyful, all along the line,
Rang the soul-stirring shout of Victory;
And wounded men came limping from the rear,   1420
To share the triumph they had help'd to win,
To see the forward march they could not join;
And at that moment, through the sulphurous clouds,
Brake out the glorious SUN, with parting ray,
Glinted from sword, and lance, and bayonet,
Gladdening the hour of triumph.

                              But behind
That line advancing, far as eye could reach,

His light gleam'd sadly on another line,

That lay unmoved, nor heard the conquering shout ;

A long red line of warriors, lock'd in sleep,   1430

Grasping their weapons, holding thus at eve

Their morning's post, which they had kept so well ;

And many a heart that leapt exulting forth,

And join'd the cheering cry of hard-won fight,

Wish'd for lost comrades now to share the joy.

But on they press, for Adam far away,

Half o'er the vale, and Cornish Vivian's horse,

Are charging onwards ; then, as Adam near'd

The ridge where yet the Guard, in square compact,

Stood rallied, up rode Wellington, and said,   1440

'*Attack at once! they will not stand;*'—'*Well done!*

'*Colborne, go on!*'—and as the line of steel

Approach'd, the square broke up, and join'd the flight.

But Vivian met with some who held their ground,

Bodies of horse, and solid infantry,

Small islands of resistance in the midst

Of that back-streaming tide. There at the head

Of one thin squadron, charging on a square
That still stood threatening, conscious of its strength,
In Victory's arms 'young gallant Howard' fell.   1450

AND where was dauntless NEY? not flying he;
But striving still to gather round him some,
Who long'd for victory, or death; his face
Dark with the smoke of many guns; his clothes
All torn by bullets; with his broken sword
Still waving o'er his head, he madly rode,
Crying aloud, '*Come! follow me, and see*
'*How dies a Marshal on the battle-field.*'
And there were acts of vengeance and despair,
The conquer'd seeking still to expiate   1460
Their deep disaster in the conquerors' blood;
And guns, that never more should fight for France,
Were fired yet once at random. One of these,
Right o'er the heads of Colborne's forward line,
Shatter'd the leg of Uxbridge—who unharm'd
Had weather'd many a deadly storm of fight,—

But did not mar his joy; '*Who would not lose*
'*A limb*,' he cried, '*for such a victory!*'

AMID the whirlwind of that driving storm
Rode Wellington, still watching; while the balls
Of friend and foe were flying all around:
And Colin Campbell warn'd him of his risk;
'*This is no place for you;*' but '*Never mind*,'
He answer'd calmly, '*let them blaze away*,'
'*The battle's won; my life is nothing now.*'
Hark! to that joyous shout! they win the line
Of cannon, that had wrought them such annoy
The livelong day; then onwards,—who shall tell
The wreck and ruin of that great defeat!
For guns abandon'd, waggons overthrown,
Munitions and camp-followings numberless,
And all the cumbrous train of wasteful war,
Block'd up the road; while soldiers of all arms,
And soldiers who had thrown their arms away,
In dread disorder struggling moved along.

YET honour still was dearer than dear life;
No Eagles there were lost; but many a time
Amid the darkening tumult rose the cry,
'Room for the colours!' never heard in vain;
The Eagles lived to gleam on brighter fields.

And still a faithful and devoted band
Closed round their Emperor, bore him safely through:
And near him still, one regiment of horse,
In firm array, moved on with stately step;
Disdain'd the foul disorder of the flight,
And scorn'd each effort to disturb their march.

Dim grew the twilight as the rout swept on;
But brightly rose the Moon; and Wellington
Recall'd his weary soldiers from the chase,
And bade them rest upon that hard-won field.

Then, as he turn'd—rejoicing to have met
And vanquish'd 'the world's victor,' crowning thus
His life-long warfare with a glorious close—

Up rode the brave old Marshal, urging on

His conquering squadrons; then were greetings glad

For toils and perils past, for Victory

So great and full; and Blucher, not content

With gratulation cold of palm to palm,

Embraced him on his horse, and kiss'd both cheeks;

While Prussian flutes and clarions sounded forth

GOD SAVE THE KING; and from both armies rang

Cheers loud and long.

        Then BLUCHER took the charge

To make their work completer, onward still

Driving the foe, and leaving him no rest,

Nor any semblance of embattled force.

AND WELLINGTON, who since the early dawn

Had watch'd and toil'd, all reckless of himself,

Rode slowly back across the battle-field,

Over the open valley; grieved at heart

For thousands of the brave, now sleeping there,

But thanking GOD for more than hoped result,

M

He reach'd his resting-place at WATERLOO;
And quick alighting at the lowly door
From Copenhagen's back, the noble horse,
Untamed by twice ten hours of glorious work,
Gave a light gladsome bound for Victory;
And shook his golden mane aloft in air;
As having help'd his lord to win the day,
And gain'd himself a name for other times.

Still'd were the storms of Heaven and Earth: the MOON   1530
Look'd calmly down upon the field of death;
The heroes slept; their blood not vainly shed;
War-wearied Europe rested forty years.

And when the peace was broken, those who fought
The fight of giants on that awful day,
With equal daring, but unequal end,
Were found in arms, and conquering, side by side,
Against the strong oppressor of the weak.

NOTES.

NOTES.

FOR the course of the battle, and for many of the descriptions, the Author is indebted to Captain Siborne's excellent History of the War in 1815: for some of the incidents, and for the two accompanying plans, to Jones' History of the Battle.

A copy of the first Edition of the Lay has been sent to every Waterloo Officer, whose address could be found, and the Author will be thankful for the address of any Waterloo Officer, or Soldier, who has not yet received a copy.

P. 5, line 80.

The English, face to face, within his grasp.

'Sa confiance dans le résultat de la journée était la même. Il voyait toujours Wellington isolé des Prussiens, et victime prochaine de la défaite la plus signalée.'

Lt.-Col. du Charras, Campagne de 1815, p. 262.

P. 5, line 83.

The boast of one that putteth harness on.

For *putteth* read *girdeth*. "Let not him that girdeth on *his harness* boast himself as he that putteth it off." I. Kings xx. 11.

P. 6, line 99.

But, had his army been the same, &c.

'If I had had my Peninsular army, I would not have fought the battle there, but at Quatre-Bras.'
Baron Gurney's Notes of Conversation with the Duke.

P. 6, line 102.

Great Massena.

'When Massena was opposed to me, and in the field, I never slept comfortably.'
S. Rogers' Recollections (Duke of Wellington), p. 201.

'I was most uneasy when I had Massena in front of me.'
Baron Gurney's Notes.

'Massena said to me (the Duke), *Vous m'avez rendu les cheveux gris.'—S. Rogers, Recollections,* p. 201.

P. 7, line 113.

Brave Craufurd sleeps upon the breach he won.

'He was buried with all military honours in the breach before which he received his mortal wound.'
Southey's Peninsular War, Vol. III. p. 404.
Siege of Ciudad Rodrigo. Jan. 19, 1812.

P. 8, lines 135, 6, 7.

Ne'er had they met, &c.

'Buonaparte I never saw; though during the battle we were once, I understood, within a quarter of a mile of each other. I regret it much; for he was a most extraordinary man.'

S. *Rogers, Recollections,* p. 208.

P. 10, line 174.

Macdonell will not leave it while he lives.

'I considered his right wing the weakest point; and Hougoumont in particular I deemed untenable in a serious assault by the enemy. This the Duke disputed, as he had put the old castle in a state of defence, and caused the long garden-wall towards the field of battle to be crenellated; and he added, "*I have thrown Macdonell into it,*" an officer on whom he placed especial reliance.'

Baron Von Müffling, Passages of my Life, p. 243.

P. 13, lines 238, 9.

Young soldiers running in that perilous game,
As late they ran in English cricket-field.

'Many of my troops were new; but the new fight well, though they manœuvre ill; better perhaps than many who have fought and bled. As to the way in which some of our ensigns and lieutenants braved danger—the boys just come from school—it exceeds all belief. They ran as at Cricket.'

S. *Rogers, Recollections,* p. 209.

Old Etonians remember a saying of the Duke's, when present at a Cricket-match in the Upper Shooting-fields, "The Battle of Waterloo was won here."

Many names of lieutenants and ensigns recorded in Jones' History of the Battle, are found in the Eton Lists of the time just preceding 1815. The lists of Harrow and other schools would probably supply many more.

P. 17, lines 309—311.

.... *As Julia came on Pompey's sleep.*

'Inde soporifero cesserunt languida somno
Membra ducis; diri tum plena horroris imago
Visa caput mæstum per hiantes Julia terras
Tollere ....

Conjuge me lætos duxisti, Magne, triumphos;
Fortuna est mutata toris.'
Lucani Pharsalia, Lib. III. init.

P. 18, line 325.

*This is the game
He loves to play;* &c.

'We talked of Napoleon's manœuvre, by which he decided so
many battles.' *Duke:* "He commenced with a pretty general firing,
"that you might not know from whence the attack was to proceed :
"then he brought forward a battery of 100 or 150 pieces of cannon,
"and, when that had swept away the troops opposed to it, he poured
"a large force into the chasm. This he had practised with success
"against every other nation ; it did not succeed with us. At Water-
"loo he played off his 100 pieces of cannon ; we did not care for
"his 100 pieces of cannon ; we did not return a shot ; we shewed
"no troops ; no persons appeared, but myself, and a few officers: I
"kept my men behind the crest of the hill, most of them lying
"down."'
Baron Gurney's Notes.

P. 40, line 739.

De Lancey bold.

'De Lancey was with me, and speaking to me, when he was
struck. We were on a point of land that overlooked the plain, and

I had just been warned off by some soldiers; 'but as I saw well from it, and as two divisions were engaging below, I had said, "Never mind" when a ball came leaping along *en ricochet*, as it is called, and striking him on the back, sent him many yards over the head of his horse. He fell on his face, and bounded upward and fell again......

'Poor fellow! we had known each other ever since we were boys. But I had no time to be sorry; I went on with the army, and never saw him again.'

'*Note*. The following remarks are in the original MS. "He said the cannon-ball was not spent, but came from quite close at hand and could not have touched. It was the wind of the shot that wounded him, no skin being broken; and mentioned another instance of a man close beside him in the trenches at   (*sic*) in India killed without being touched."'

S. Rogers, Recollections, p. 210.

P. 40, lines 749, 50.

His own brave chestnut, at the rushing whiz,
So sharp and shrill, uneasy paws the ground;

(The Duke) 'A horse will wince when a ball makes a noise like this (imitating the sound), but when he hears it the danger is past.'
S. Rogers, Recollections, p. 211, note.

P. 43, line 802.

Poor Cooke! he's gone!

Lieut-Colonel Richard Harvey Cooke, then Captain in the Grenadier Guards. He lived till 1856, and was one of the guests at the Duke's last Waterloo Banquet, June 18, 1852.

Allix (afterwards Colonel Allix), then Captain and Adjutant in the Grenadier Guards, also lived to the age of 80, at Swaffham Prior, Cambs.

P. 49, line 922.

Brave Ellis, their Commander.

'As the day advanced, Colonel Sir Henry Ellis, perceiving an opening where his regiment might be employed with advantage, moved it up into the line ; where, formed in square, it sustained several charges of the French Cuirassiers. The greater numbers of the men were now, for the first time, in presence of an enemy : but these emulated the steadiness of their veteran comrades, and all nobly maintained the character of the regiment.'

'The glories of the battle of Waterloo were however dearly purchased by the Royal Welsh Fusiliers with the life of their beloved commander, Sir Henry Ellis, who, continuing on horseback in the centre of the square, was struck with a musket-ball in the right breast. Feeling himself faint from loss of blood, he calmly desired an opening might be made in the square, and rode to the rear. At a short distance from the field he was thrown from his horse, while in the act of leaping a ditch ; here he was found soon afterwards much exhausted, and conveyed to a neighbouring outhouse, where his wound was dressed. In the course of the night of the 19th, the hovel in which he was lodged unfortunately caught fire, and he was with difficulty rescued from the flames by Assistant-Surgeon Munro, of the regiment, but exhausted by so many shocks, he soon after expired, (aged 32). The Regiment erected a tablet to his memory in the Church of Waterloo, and a monument at a cost of 1200/. in the Cathedral of Worcester, his native city.'

Historical Record of the 23rd Foot, 1847, p. 153.

P. 53, line 985.

The Prussian Baron.

Baron von Müffling, Quartermaster-General of the Prussian army, sent to the English Head-Quarters, to keep up the connexion between the Duke of Wellington and Field-marshal Blucher. He died at his estate near Erfurt, Jan. 16, 1851, aged 77.

P. 53, line 990.

You see, Macdonell still holds Hougoumont.

'I met the Duke in the neighbourhood of Haye la Sainte, holding a telescope raised in his right hand: he called out to me from a distance: "Well! you see Macdonell has held Hougoumont!"'

Baron Müffling. p. 249.

P. 54, lines 1009, 10.

Where would he have me find them? does he think
That I can call up soldiers from the ground?

'De l'infanterie! où voulez-vous que j'en prenne? Voulez-vous que j'en fasse?'

Lt.-Colonel Charras, Campagne de 1815, p. 296.

P. 54, line 1015.

Oftimes the British Leader watch'd the hour.

'A friend of ours had the courage to ask the Duke of Wellington, whether in that conjuncture he looked often to the woods from which the Prussians were expected to issue, "No," was the answer, "I looked oftener at my watch than at anything else: I knew if my troops could keep their position till night, that I must be joined by Blucher before morning, and we would not have left Buonaparte an army next day. But," continued he, "I own I was glad as one hour of daylight slipped away after another, and our position was still maintained."'

Paul's Letters to his Kinsfolk, (by Sir W. Scott,) p. 175.

P. 55, line 1034.

The battle-thunder borne across the sea.

In a note to the Correspondence between Sir Isaac Newton and Professor Cotes, (p. xlvii.) the Editor (J. Edleston) quotes from Nichols's History of Hinckley the following tradition of the noise of battle, borne from Southwold Bay to Cambridge, May 28, 1672.

"'There is a traditional story at Cambridge...[that] Sir Isaac Newton came into the hall of Trinity College and told the other fellows that there had been an action just then between the Dutch and English, and that the latter had the worst of it. Being asked how he came by his knowledge, he said that being in the observatory, he heard the report of a great firing of cannon, such as could only be between two great fleets, and that as the noise grew louder and louder he concluded that they drew nearer to our coasts, and consequently that we had the worst of it, which the event verified.' Jones, in his *Physiological Disquisitions*, p. 299 (quoted *ib.*), says that he had been informed 'that the great engagement between the Dutch and English at sea in 1672 was heard by the people who were out at work in the fields to the very centre of England: Mr Derham says it was heard 200 miles.' The 'observatory' in the passage quoted above is a prolepsis for the 'great gateway,' which was not converted into an observatory until several years after Newton had left Cambridge."

P. 62, lines 1164, 5.

He sends his horsemen spurring through the field,
To spread the tidings wish'd for, but not true.

"A droite, au contraire, du coté de Frichemont, la canonnade redoublait, toute l'affaire semblait s'être portée là-bas, et l'on n'osait pas se dire; 'Ce sont les Prussiens qui vous attaquent...une armée de plus qui vient vous écraser!' Non, cette idée vous paraissait trop épouvantable, quand tout-à-coup un officier d'état-major passa comme un éclair en criant :
'*Grouchy!...le Maréchal Grouchy arrive!*'"
Waterloo. *Erckmann-Chatrian*, Paris.

P. 81, line 1512.

Embraced him on his horse, and kiss'd both cheeks.

'When all was over, Blucher and I met at La Maison Rouge. It was midnight when he came; and riding up, he threw his arms round me, and kissed me on both cheeks as I sat in the saddle. I was then in pursuit; and, as his troops were fresh, I halted mine, and left the business to him.'

S. Rogers, p. 212.

'*It happens that the meeting took place after ten at night, at the village of Genappe;* and any body who attempts to describe with truth the operations of the different armies will see that *it could not be otherwise* ... in truth, I was not off my horse till I returned to Waterloo between eleven and twelve at night.

Wellington Dispatches, Vol. VIII. p. 332.

'I asked, whether the story was true of his having ridden over to Blucher the night before the battle of Waterloo, and returned on the same horse?

'*Duke.* No! that was not so. I did not see Blucher the day before Waterloo; I saw him the day before (or the day of) Quatre-Bras.

'I saw him after Waterloo, and he kissed me; he embraced me on horseback. I *communicated* with him the day before Waterloo.'

Baron Gurney's Notes.

P. 82, line 1527, 8.

From Copenhagen's back, the noble horse,
Untamed by twice ten hours of glorious work.

On that day I rode Copenhagen from four in the morning till twelve at night. And when I dismounted he threw up his heels at me as he went off. If he fed, it was on the standing corn, and as I sat in the saddle. He was a chestnut horse. I rode him hundreds of miles in Spain, and at the battle of Toulouse. He died blind with age—28 years old—in 1835, at Strathfieldsaye, where he lies buried within a ring fence.'

S. Rogers, p. 212.

CAMBRIDGE: PRINTED AT THE UNIVERSITY PRESS.

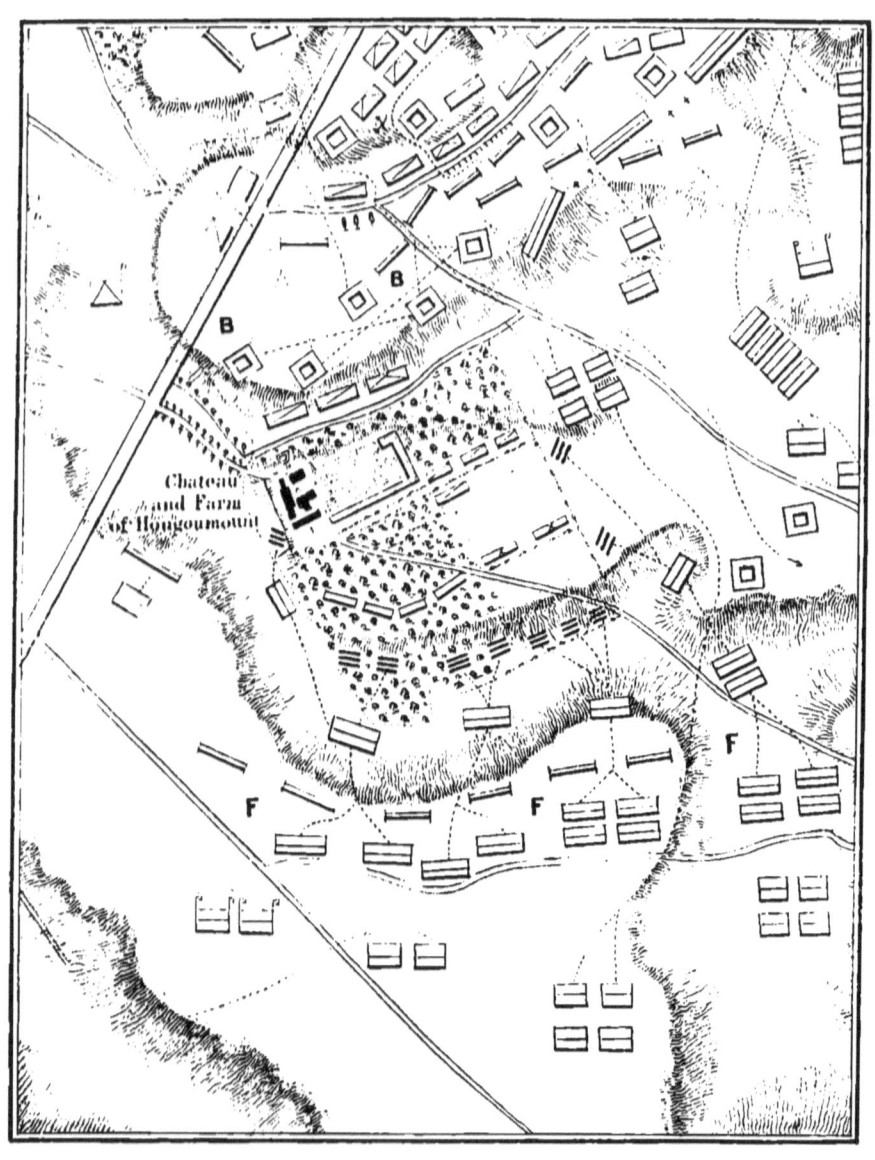

B. B. *British Position*   F. F. *French Position*.

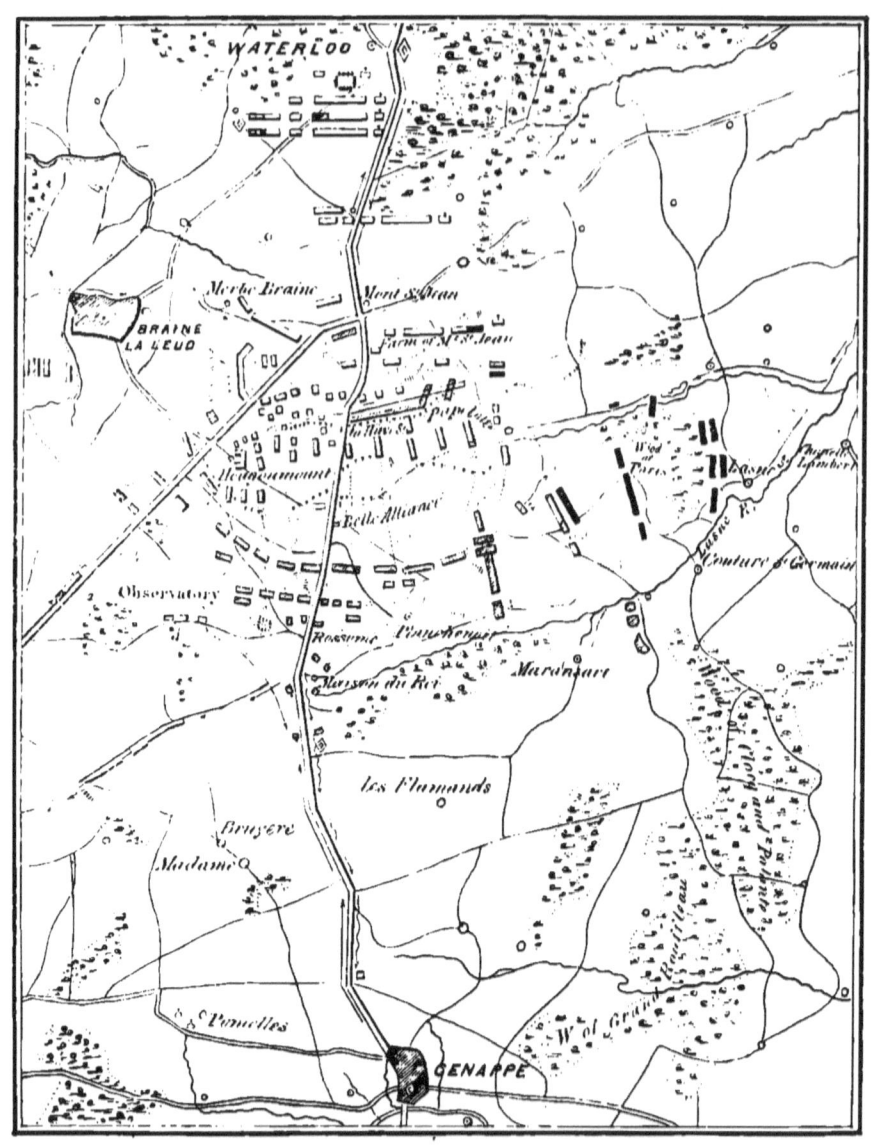

English Army ☐   French Army ▨   Prussian Army ▬

ENOCHVS ARDEN

Cantabrigiæ:

TYPIS ACADEMICIS C. J. CLAY, A.M.

ENOCH ARDEN

POEMA TENNYSONIANVM

LATINE REDDITVM

Londini
EDV. MOXON ET SOC:
A.D.
M. DCCCLXVII.

IN
MEMORIAM
GVLIELMI SELWYN
PATRIS OPTIMI
QVI HÆC STVDIA
AMAVIT ADOLESCENS
FOVIT SENEX
FILIVS AMANTISSIMVS.

L. B.

Accipe, quæ nuper, casu dejectus iniquo,
Æger adhuc, semperque dolorum oblivia quærens,
In lecto meditabar; habens in mente reposta
Eximii vatis, frontem cui laurea cingit,
Carmina; quæ mecum recolens, taciteque revolvens
Longas insomnis gaudebam fallere noctes.

Nox autem una fuit, medio fere mense Novembri,
Quæ sanos ægrosque simul spectare coëgit
Mirifico splendore ruentia sidera cœli.

Si qua notes longo culpanda in carmine; si qua
Archetypæ invenias male respondentia chartæ,
Judicio leni, velut ægri somnia, penses:
Forsitan et tua te docet experientia, sensum
Subtilem, et magni felicia verba poetæ,
Multaque temporibus non convenientia priscis,
"Difficile illustrare Latinis versibus esse."

DOMINO PROCANCELLARIO

ET

ACADEMIÆ CANTABRIGIENSI.

VOBIS exopto, quâ non fruor ipse, salutem,
Effundens almâ pro genitrice preces;
Languidus, e lecto; sed non languentia vota;
Ægroti insolito corda calore tument.

O Patres, Fratresque, sacratæ Lucis alumni,
Non leve momentum est, quod tulit una dies[1]:
Plena inter vitæ commercia, plena laborum
Tempora, ad æternas procubuisse fores;
Et subito lethi affinem sensisse soporem;
Hæc sunt queis animum tangit ad ima DEUS.

Vidi etenim, lapsu quamvis confusus iniquo,
Quam vigil et fervens iste Paternus Amor;
Qui regit errantes stellas moderamine summo,
Et sine quo passer nullus in arva cadit.
Et sensi, fratrum pietas, e fonte perenni,
Quam læto arentes irriget amne locos.

[1] November 10, 1866.

O utinam grates possem persolvere dignas,

Vobis qui e durâ me relevâstis humo[1]:

Vobis qui curâ vigilanti, atque arte medendi[2],

Fovistis læsi membra caputque viri:

Vobis, quos scalâ angelicâ conscendere cœlum,

Et laticem ex AGNI promere fonte juvat.

Et tu, qui, juvenum rapidissime, non ita justo

Tramite, seu nimium præpete raptus equo,

Sive ipse impellens, lapsûs mihi causa fuisti;

Tu mihi, sub DOMINO, causa quietis, ave!

Sed precor, hoc posthac reminiscere; *carpe sinistram;*

Dextram occurrenti linquere norma jubet.

Omnibus ex animo grates! det MAXIMUS ILLE

Omnibus æterna luce et amore frui.

GULIELMUS SELWYN,

DOM. MARGARETÆ IN SACRA THEOLOGIA LECTOR.

Nov. 20, A. D. 1866.

---

[1] W. Kennedy, King's Coll.
Ravenscroft Stewart, Trin. Coll.
W. H. Anable, ⎫ of the Pitt Press.
J. Halls, ⎭

[2] G. E. Paget, M.D. Caius Coll.
C. Lestourgeon, M.A. Trin. Coll.

LITOREÆ rupes ubi fissæ in chasma recedunt,

Spumâque Oceanus flavas conspergit arenas,

Angustum circa portum stant tegmina rubra

Confertim, templumque vetustum ; hinc scandere cœpit

Vicus ad excelsa dominantem turre molinam ;

Altiùs, in cœlo, clivi juga cana supini,

Consita · Danorum tumulis ; et grata juventæ

Silva, nucum genitrix, autumni tempore læto,

Anfraƈtum clivi viridanti vestit amiƈtu.

Centum abiere anni, ex quo lusit littore in isto   10

Parva trias, tribus ex domibus; formosa puella,

Filiolas inter parvi pulcherrima portûs,

Annia, Laiorum de stirpe; puerque Philippus,

Raiorum soboles, altæ spes una molinæ;

Enochusque, orbum genitor quem fecerat, Arden,

Naufragus hibernis in fluctibus; hasce per oras,

Hos inter cumulos, disjectos litore in udo,

Retia jam fuscata mari, durosque rudentes,

Qua lintres inter subductos scabra jacebat

Anchora, munibant castella madentis arenæ,   20

Spe redeuntis aquæ; et pelagi cristata sequentes

Agmina, vel rursus fugientes, tenuia passim

Linquebant delenda salo vestigia primo.

Cernis ubi angustum penetrat sub rupibus antrum?

Hic pueri hospitium tenuere, alterna vicissim

Jura exercentes; dominäi munera semper

Annia complebat; sed forti corpore pollens

Interdum Enochus per sabbata tota tenebat

Imperium; *hæc domus est mea, et hæc mea parvula conjux:*

Et mea clamavit *par lex utrique* Philippus; 30

Tum rixæ, Enocho semper victore; Philippus,

Cæruleos largo lacrymarum flumine ocellos

Exundans, sævire odio; dum parvula conjux

Fletibus ac precibus satagens componere lites,

Uxorem sese puero spondebat utrique.

Mox ubi, jam vitæ puerili flore peracto,

Cœpit in ambobus pariter nova flamma calere;

Virgine in hac unâ defixus fervet uterque;

Acrior Enochus linguâ declarat amorem,

Alter amat tacitè; virgoque favere Philippo 40

Visa quidem, Enochum vixdum sibi conscia, amavit;

Sæpe rogata negans. Operi se devovet uni

Enochus, summâ quæ possit cogere curâ,

Mercarique sibi lintrem, casulamque parare

Uxori optatæ; tam felix ille laborum,

Fortior haud alius, nec fortunatior usquam

Piscator, meliùsve sagax urgente periclo,

Sulcabat fluctus in litora longa furentes.

Quinetiam integrum in ponto compleverat annum,

Ediscens artem; sic pleno jure potitus 50

Navita; robustâque manu servarat ab undis

Bis terque horrendo raptam sub gurgite vitam:

Egregieque illum vicinia tota colebat.

Nec prius attigerat bis denos providus annos,

Quam sibi navigium emisset, casulamque parasset

Uxori optatæ, modico sub tegmine nidum,

In medio ad celsam vico scandente molinam.

Evocat interea ad corylos de more popellum

Aurea tempestas autumni; et vespere læto

Magna cohors juvenum, saccis et onusta canistris, 60

Egreditur, raptura nuces: sed patre Philippum

Ægrotante domi pietas retinebat in horam;

Tum clivum scandens, ubi prono limite silva

Vergit in anfraCtum, fixus stetit: ecce sedebant

Molliter implicitis Enochus et Annia dextris;

Enochi facies durata, et cæsia flammâ

Lumina flagrabant sacrâ, velut ignis in arâ

Numinis accensi; videt, agnoscitque Philippus

Amborum ex oculis, præsago pectore, fatum:

Utque genæ accessit propior gena, pectore toto

Ingemuit; pedibusque aversis intima, qualis

Cerva gerens vulnus, silvæ in penetralia repsit;

Dumque alii implebant lætis clamoribus umbras,

Solus ibi tenebras luctumque fovebat amarum;

Evasitque famem diuturnam in pectore celans.

Conjugio pacto, campanæ læta sonabant;

Læti currebant anni, feliciter anni

Septeni; nec firma salus, nec copia rerum

Defuit, ingenuum studio fallente laborem;

Prima viro movit vagitu infantula primo

Nobile consilium, curâ asservare fideli

Omnigenos quæstus; ut posset parvula nata

Quæ non contigerat matrive, patrive, doceri;

Crevit et hoc votum, cum mox vicesima volvens

Luna tulit puerum, genitrici dulce periclum,

Cùm sæpe, Enocho iratas errante per undas,

Vel terras obeunte, domi Annia sola sederet.

Albus enim Enochi gravidâ cum corbe caballus,

Oceani spolia, Oceanum redolentia late,

Et vultus vento scaber atque hiemalibus undis,   90

Vix meliùs fuerant vicino cognita pago,

Quam procul umbrosis in callibus, ulteriora

Trans juga, qua catulo stat custodita leonis

Aula vetus, taxi pavonem imitantis in umbra;

Victum jejunis ubi præbuit ille diebus.

Nunc subiere vices (ea sors communis ubique;)

Haud procul angusto a portu, Borealia versus,

Largior incurrit sinus; illuc ire solebat

Enochus, terrâve marive, negotia curans;

Hic, malum in portu scandens, pede lapsus ab alto   100

Decidit in puppim; quem fracto crure tulerunt;

Invalidusque diu jacuit; dum tertia proles

Nata domi est, infans male debilis; et simul alter

Surripit Enochi quæstus, unde Annia victum

Et soboles habuere; et quamvis ille serenâ

Cum gravitate Deum et submisso corde colebat,
Cura virum tamen et caligo oppressit inertem.

Vidit, (ut in somnis cum somnia læva fatigant
Ægrotum) dulces natos miseranda trahentes
Tempora, solicitos quid cras sibi restet edendum;   110
Mendicam uxorem: tum toto corde precatur,
Hæc Deus avertat, mala sint mihi quælibet ipsi ;
Vix prece finitâ, navis venit ecce magister,
Quo duce servierat, casum miseratus iniquum,
(Nôrat enim Enochum, et pretii non vilis habebat,)
Navigium memorans ad Serica litora iturum;
Deficiente tamen proretâ; *quid tibi visum?*
Tempus adhuc restat quod sufficit; evehimurque
Hoc ipso ex portu; si te juvet ire, videto:
Enochus studio promptissimus annuit, *ibo;*   120
Lætus, quod voti compos feliciter esset.

Atque ita nil gravius visa est gravis umbra doloris,
Quam cum flagrantem Solis nubecula lucem

Abscindit propiùs, dum splendet lumine pontus
Ulterior;—sed quid tenerâ de conjuge fiet?
De pueris? sine patre—marito—quid faciendum?
Noctes atque dies jacuit, secum omnia volvens:
Vendendus linter? sed lintrem totus amavit;
Præruptos quoties fluctus superarat in illo!
Miles equum veluti, dilexit navita lintrem: 130
Vendere sed constat tandem, pretioque recepto,
Omnigenas merces, quas Annia vendat, emendas;
Quicquid erit nautis—uxoribus—utile, vendat;
Sic poterit casulam servare absente marito.
Ipse ego, nonne geram longe hinc commercia? pontum
Transcurram vice plus unâ? demumque revertens
Dives opum, cymbæ dominus melioris, habebo
Majores quæstus, levioris præmia vitæ;
Omnia tum nati discent, quæ discere prosit;
Ipse meos inter transibo leniter ævum.   140

Sic secum Enochus statuit rem fervidus omnem;
Inde domum rediens uxori intervenit; illa

Pallens, infantemque fovens amplexibus ægrum,
Prosiluit, lætam rumpens e pectore vocem ;
Et dedit infantem tenerum genitoris in ulnas ;
Qui puerum laudans tractavit amore paterno
Invalidos artus, et quanti ponderis esset
Conjecit ; sed non potuit nova promere verbis
Consilia ; hæc demum patefecit luce sequenti.

Primùm tunc, ex quo digitum sibi cinxerat auro
Annulus Enochi, obnixè stetit Annia contra ;
Venturos etenim vidit præsaga dolores ;
At non multa loquens, nec amaris illa querelis,
Sed prece multiplici lacrymisque frequentibus urgens,
Osculaque ingeminans noctuque dieque, maritum
Orabat supplex, si quid pietatis haberet,
Ne se, ne dulces pueros ita linqueret orbos.
Ille nihil pro se, totam pro conjuge curam
Exercens, puerisque, preces permisit inanes,
Propositumque dolens tenuit, pleneque peregit.

Vendidit Enochus lintrem, quem totus amavit,
Omnigenasque emit merces, uxoris in usum,
Et cameram instruxit tenuem, quæ proxima vico,
Cellis ac pluteis, ubi merces rite jacerent.
Jamque dies totos, donec supremus adesset
Ante abitum Enochi, casulam quassabat amœnam
Malleus, et serræ stridor gravis; illa sibi ipsi
Credidit interea mortis tabulata parari:
Tandem opus exaêtum est; Enochi callida dextra
Angustis spatiis merces aptaverat omnes,
Vix minus exaêtè quam tenuia germina claudit
Natura in loculis; tum demum desiit, ut qui
Parcere ne minimæ voluit pro conjuge curæ,
Lassusque ascendens in lucem dormiit altam.

Mane novo cum jam conjux linquenda, domusque,
Ille hilaris fortisque fuit; quot quanta timeret
Annia, ridebat, si non tam cara fuisset;
Sed quoniam DOMINUM summâ gravitate colebat,
Enochus genibus flexis secreta recludens

Pectora, quà coeunt divina humanaque in unum,

Uxori et pueris cælestia dona precatur,

Quælibet eveniant ipsi ; dein talia profert;

Annia, si faveat Dominus, dum currimus æquor,

Proderit hoc nobis, melioraque tempora fient.

Splendeat iste focus ; casulam mihi provida serva ;

Et priùs ipsa virum quam expectes, cara, redibo.

Inde agitans leviter pueri cunabula, *Et ille,*

Debilis, ægrotus, sed formosissimus infans,—

Et quia debilior, tanto mihi carior ille,—

Det DEUS, *ut felix posthâc genitore reverso*

Insideat genibus, dum quæ miracula abundent

Trans maria auscultans, avidas vix expleat aures :

Annia, pone metus, animumque recollige fortem.

Talia dum fudit spe fervidus, audiit illa,

Ipsa velut sperans: sed cùm, graviora capessens,

Nautarum ritu, cœpit sermonibus uti,

De vigilante DEO ut bene sit fidentibus Ipsi,

Auribus, haud animo, percepit verba : puella

Rustica ceu vivo urceolum sub fonte reponit,
Et juvenem meditans qui quondam implere solebat,
Audit, non audit, dum lympha superfluit oras.

Tum fatur; *Semper sapiens, Enoche, fuisti,*
Sed quævis tua sit sapientia, res mihi certa est;
His oculis posthac non aspiciendus abibis.

Siccine? respondit, *certè tamen aspiciam te;*
Et tu—nostra ratis prælabitur, Annia, portum
Mane, die quarto—cape tu prospectile vitrum,
Explora hanc faciem, et vanos dispelle timores.

Cùm vero extremam tempus fugisset ad horam,
Annia! sis animo forti; solatia quære;
Tu cura pueros, et donec me tibi reddam,
Omnia rite tene; nunc instat tempus; eundum est;
Nil de me timeas; vel si timor ingruat, omnes
Mitte DEO *curas; nunquam anchora deficit illa.*
Nonne DEUS *partes illas Orientis adusti*

Occupat extremas? illuc si deferar, Illum
Effugere haud potero: Maria omnia possidet Ille,
Ille creavit aquas.

Tum surgit, certus eundi,
Fortia circumdans uxori brachia lapsæ,
Osculaque attonitis infigens ultima natis;
Sed qui sopitus cunis, infantulus æger,
Post noctem insomni vexatam febre jacebat;
Annia cum relevare pararet, noluit ille;
Ne moveas; dormire sinas; meminisse diei
Infans qui poterit? clausisque dat oscula ocellis.
Annia cincinnum tenuem de fronte puelli
Decerpens dat—triste!—viro; quem collocat ille
In gremio; amplexusque uxorem, fasciculumque
Arripiens, dextrâ valedicit, iterque capessit.

Illa die quarto, cum navis raderet oras,
Explorat vitro; sed frustrà; sive nequiret
Aptare insolito vitrum, cum vellet, ocello;

Seu manibus tremor, aut oculis offecerit humor;

Cernere non potuit; dum dextram commovet ille

E puppi, navis cita præterit, effugit hora.

Donec supremum vidit vanescere velum,

Invigilat, repetitque domum lacrimosa reliftam;

Tum, licet absentem quasi raptum funere fleret,

Mœsta voluntatem studuit complere mariti;

Sed nil profecit; non illa assueta negotî   240

Artibus, ingeniove artem supplere parata;

Non fuci, fraudisve capax; nec poscere callens

Quod nimium, pretio demum contenta minori;

Et semper secum reputans, quid diceret ille?

Nam vice plus unâ, torquentibus obruta curis,

Dum gravis ingrueret paupertas, Annia merces

Vendidit haud tanti, quanti prius emerat ipsa;

Rem minui sensit paulatim, crescere curas;

Et non venturam sperans de conjuge famam,

Ipsa sibi tenuem vidum, puerisque parabat,   250

Producens tacito vitam tristissima luftu.

Tertius ille infans, ex ortu debilis, ibat

In pejus, quanquam maternâ sedula curâ

Omnia quæ fieri potuerunt Annia fecit ;

Seu quia sæpe aliàs traxere negotia matrem,

Seu quia non, morbum quod fallere posset, habebat ;

Vel quòd tum medico pro doctâ voce nequiret

Solvere quod solitum ; quid præcipitaverit, anceps ;

Sensim languescens, cum nil ea tale timeret,

Evolat ut claustro volucris captiva repente,   260

Vita tenellula pura suas evasit in auras.

Jam quintus postquam sepeliverat Annia natum

Vesper erat, cum corde pio veroque Philippus

Exoptans illi pacem, et felicia cuncta,

(Ex abitu Enochi prudens non viderat illam)

Culpavit sese, quod tam diuturnus abesset.

Nunc illam certè liceat mihi visere, dixit ;

Solari paullum possim ; sic ille locutus,

Intrans per cameram vacuam, quæ proxima vico,

Substitit interiùs, dubitans ; paullumque moratus   270

Pulsavit bis, terque : et cùm vox nulla reponat,

Ingreditur; sed sola sedens, intenta dolori,

Annia, quippe recens ab acerbo funere nati,

Non valuit quemquam coram spectare ; sed ipsa

Aversâ facie lacrymas stillabat amaras ;

Accedens propius tremulâ sic voce Philippus,

Annia ! paulisper faveas, unumque rogabo.

Dixerat ; illa gemens, ingenti concita luctu,

Mene rogare aliquid? me tam miseram atque relictam?

Obstupuit pavidus ; sed mox, licet illa taceret,   280

Dum pudor et pietas urgebant corda vicissim,

Assedit lateri, compellans voce benignâ :

Pauca velim fari; notum est quid semper averet

Vir tuus, Enochus; solitus sum sæpe fateri,

Te nupsisse viro, inter nos fortissimus omnes

Qui foret ; ille animo quicquid statuisset agendum,

Fortiter imposuit dextram, pleneque peregit :

Et quo nunc motus longinquum navigat æquor,

Te plorante domi? studio loca multa videndi ?

Ut se delectet? nihil hoc; sed amore lucrandi   290

Quo melius possit soboles dilecta doceri,

Quàm vestrûm alteruter; solum hoc sibi destinat ille.

Et si forte domum remcârit, crede, dolebit,

Perdita cùm nôrit vernantis tempora vitæ;

Atque etiam in terrâ vexabit cura sepultum,

Si natos sciat incultos sine lege vagari,

Ceu pullos juga per deserta; eia! Annia, quæso,

—Nonne ego te, tu me, a primis jam novimus annis?—

Per quem tam fido coluisti semper amore,

Per pueros, ne me poscentem aversa repellas—   300

Nam, si fert animus, cum rursus venerit ille,

Omnia restituet,—modo sic tibi certa voluntas,

Annia—nam largus rerum mihi suppetit usus:

Eia! sine ad ludum puerum mittam, atque puellam;

Hoc unum est quod me dixi te velle rogare.

Annia mœsta, premens adverso pariete frontem,

Respondit; *non possum oculos attollere coram;*

Me miseram, sum fracta adeo, labefactaque prorsus;

Ut primum intrâsti, dolor acer me labefecit;
Nunc verò rursus bonitas tua me labefactat;   310
Sed meus Enochus vivit—certum id mihi constat—
Et tibi restituet; mera possunt æra rependi;
Gratia tanta nequit.

        Leni tum voce Philippus,

Annia, concedesne igitur?

        Conversa repente
Surrexit, spectans oculis manantibus illum,
Paulisper faciem perlegit fixa benignam,
Implorans illi de cælo dona faventi,
Arripiensque manum compressit fervida; deinde,
Præpes in areolam retro sublapsa refugit;
Atque animo elatus celsam petit ille molinam.   320

    Protinus ad ludum mittit puerum atque puellam,
Suppeditat libros, et in omnibus, haud aliter quàm
Fungitur officio genitor, propriosque tuetur,

Illis se tradit ; tencrâ formidine verò,

Annia ne levis oppeteret convicia vulgi,

Sæpe pedem, votumque ante omnia dulce repressit,

Et rarò casulam intravit ; sed munera multa

Per pueros, fruêtus horti, vel oluscula, misit ;

Primas vere rosas, serosque æstatis honores ;

A clivo leporem ; quandoque, at parciùs illud,   330

Prætendens aliquid rari in similagine purâ,

Ne forte offensam pareret bonitate, farinam

E celsâ et latè circum stridente molinâ.

Femineam verò mentem penetrare Philippus

Noñ potuit ; quoties interfuit, Annia pleno

Peêtore, et immensâ meritorum mole laborans,

Vix habuit vocem, grates quâ solveret, unam :

Cum pueris autem punêtum tulit omne Philippus ;

Currebant vici longinquo a limite, lætâ

Voce salutantes lætâ qui voce vocavit ;   340

Imperiumque domûs et celsæ habuere molinæ ;

Sollicitaverunt patientem questibus aurem,

Et precibus; patrem vocitabant; lusibus illum
Implicuere suis: sic carior esse Philippus,
Inque diem propior fieri; sic cedere retro
Enochus semper; neque erat jam certior illis
Enochus, quam vana animum quæ ludit imago
In somnis; vel cùm sublustri mane videtur
Forma viri longè silvarum rara sub umbrâ,
Vanescens dubiè; decimus sic vertitur annus,   350
Ex quo dilectam casulam patriamque reliquit
Enochus; sed nulla absentis nuntia fama.

Forte, iterum nucibus maturis, vespere festo
Annia promisit pueris, cupientibus ire
Ad corylos, sese simul affore; tum rogitârunt
Ut sineret secum '*patrem*' sociare '*Philippum:*'
Illum, apis in morem perfusæ polline florum,
Albentem farre inveniunt; multumque rogatus,
'*Eia! Philippe pater, venias simul,*' ille recusat;
Ut vero prensare manu cœpere, trahentes,   360
Risit, et assensum facilem dedit—Annia mater
Stabat cum pueris—ad silvam protinus itur.

Cum verò medium cœpissent scandere clivum,

Haud procul a corylis, ubi prono limite silva

Vergit in anfraɛtum, sibi vires Annia sensit

Prorsus deficere; et *sine*, mùrmurat illa, *quiescam :*

Asseditque, suâ contentus sorte, Philippus.

Multiplici intereà exultans clamore juventus,

Elapsa ex manibus seniorum, effusa tumultu,

Per corylos albescentes, in concava silvæ   37ɔ

Ima ruit; sparsique dolentes cedere ramos

Fleɛtunt certatim, aut frangunt, fulvosque corymbos

Deripiunt, socios alternâ voce vocantes,

Complentesque hilari late nemus omne loquelâ.

Lætitiæ verò præsentis pæne Philippus

Immemor, unam illam recolit lugubriter horam,

Hàc ipsâ in silvâ, cùm qualis saucia cerva,

Cessit in umbrarum latebras; tum fatur, honestam

Attollens frontem, paullò jucundiùs, *Audin'?*

Annia! quam lætis resonent clamoribus umbræ.   38ɔ

Annia! lassa adeò? nam vocem haud reddidit ullam;

Lassa ? sed in palmas facies delapsa quievit ;

Tum, quasi vix iram cohibens in corde, Philippus,

Abjecta est navis, dixit ; *desiste querelis ;*

Abjecta est navis ; num vis te absumere luctu,

Et pueros orbos penitus facere ? Annia verò ;

Non illud versabam animo ; sed, nescio quare,

Vocibus admoneor lætis, quàm sola relinquar.

Accedens propiùs leni sic voce Philippus ;

Annia, pauca loquar ; res est mihi mente repôsta, 390

Tamque diu tacito celata in pectore mansit,

Ut, quamvis nequeam revocare ab origine primâ,

Non fieri possit, quin prodeat. Annia, fabor ;

Extra spem positum est, humanâ sorte negatum,

Illum, qui denos absit, jamque amplius, annos,

Vivere adhuc ; agedum, liceat mihi pauca profari ;

Te spectare inopem doleo, adjutore carentem ;

Nec possum tibi opem quam vellem ferre, tuisque,

Te nisi—sed quoniam præsentit femina semper,

Novisti forsan quod nunc tibi dicere conor ; 400

23

Te cupio uxorem. Pueros erga hosce libenter

Muneribus fungar patriis; et credere fas est

Illis me carum, ac si essem pater; Hoc scio certè,

Me, veluti soboles essent mea, diligere illos:

Et mihi persuasum est, si te mihi jungere velles

Connubio, post hæc incerta et tristia vitæ

Tempora, possemus felices vivere, quantum

Dat Deus in terris. Hæc, Annia, mente revolve;

Nam mihi res ampla est; sine curâ—fœnoris expers;

Nil, nisi cura tui, quod me gravet, atque tuorum; 410

Nonne ego te, tu me, a primis jam novimus annis?

Et plures annos ego te quàm credis amavi.

Annia respondens tenero sic corde profatur;

Angelus e cælo tu semper, amice, fuisti,

Tegmine sub nostro; Dominus tibi rite rependat,

Atque aliquid donet longè felicius, oro;

An bis amare datur? tu, credin'? amaberis unquam,

Ceu prior Enochus? quid proderit, esse quod optas?

Ille, nihil metuens; *Bene sum contentus amari*

Paulò post Enochum. Illa hoc quasi territa verbo, 420

O parce! exclamat, *paulisper, care Philippe;*
Enocho redeunte—sed heu! nunquam ille redibit—
Annum cede tamen, quæso; cito vertitur annus;
Elapso certè fiam sapientior anno;
Expecta paulum! Tristi tum voce Philippus,
Annia, qui vitam expectando pertulit omnem,
Fas expectet adhuc. *Mihi fidas,* Annia clamat,
Constringor, pepigi venientem fœdus in annum;
Nonne pari mecum tu sorte manebis in annum?
Annum ego, respondit, sed tristiùs, ille, *manebo.*   430

Conticuere ambo; donec sursum ora Philippus
Attollens, lapsi morientia lumina Solis
Danorum a tumulis sensim vanescere vidit:
Tum, vespertinum ne carperet Annia frigus,
Surrexit, vocemque cavas demisit in umbras,
Et pueros silvæ spoliis revocavit onustos;
Fit brevis ad portum descensus; ibique Philippus
Substitit ad limen casulæ, dextrâque prehensâ,
Leniter alloquitur; *tibi cum mea vota profarer,*

Annia, tu fueras labefacta; ignosce locuto;   044
Constringor tibi perpetuo; tu libera restas.
Annia tum lacrimans, *Constringor fœdere pacto.*

Dixerat: et veluti momento temporis uno,
Dum satagebat adhuc curis intenta diurnis,
Dum volvebat adhuc secum ultima verba Philippi,
Quod plures annos illam, quàm sciret, amâsset;
Ecce iterum Autumni tempestas aurea fulsit,
Atque iterum attonitæ stetit illi ante ora Philippus,
Promissum repetens. *Annus fugitne?* rogavit;
Si qua fides nucibus maturescentibus, ille;   450
Egredere, ut videas. Ast illa elusit amantem;
Tot facienda prius—mutanda fere omnia—mensem,
Cede mihi mensem—constringor fœdere pacto—
Mensem—nil ultra. Tremulâ tum voce Philippus,
(Ceu cum populeam movet aura levissima frondem)
Sicca fame nunquam satiandâ lumina figens;
Sume tibi quantum placeat—sume, Annia, tempus.
Annia vix lacrimas reprimit, miserata dolentem:

4

Attamen optatam cunétando distulit horam,

Et vix credibiles neétebat pendula causas,　　　　　　460

Explorare fidem, et longum quasi vellet amorem,

Dum vernis iterum recreat se floribus annus.

Interea angusti vicinia garrula portûs,

Non tolerans frustrata diu præsagia, cœpit

Accepto veluti stomachari et fervere damno:

Nil nisi nugari quidam dixere *Philippum;*

Illam alii *differre, ut spe laétaret amantem:*

Et multi risere illam, risere Philippum,

Ceu fatuos qui non quid vellent sat bene nossent:

Unus item, qui prava animo commenta fovebat,　　　470

Serpentum velut ova tenaci interlita visco,

Pejus utrique aliquid risu intentabat amaro.

Filius, ore tacens, oculis facundior orat;

Sed prece perpetuâ genitricem nata fatigat,

Nubere velle viro, qui carior omnibus esset,

Pauperiemque foras, et edaces pellere curas.

Pallere interea facies rubicunda Philippi,

Et rugæ signare genas; atque Annia sensit

Ceu culpæ stimulo cruciari pectora.

Tandem

Nocte sub obscurâ insomnis jacet Annia, totâ   •   480

Mente petens signum; *Evasitne Enochus in auras?*

Tum, cæco noctis veluti circumdata muro,

Non valuit cordis præsagum ferre pavorem;

Prosiluit lecto—scintillam excudit—et amens

Arripuit sacrum, fuit hæc spes ultima, Librum;

Explicuit subito, optati cupidissima signi;

Et subito digitum vocem defixit in illam,

Sub palmâ. Nihil hoc: dubiæ hoc solatia menti

Nulla dedit; clauso Libro, sopita quievit.

Ecce autem ENOCHUS, clivo sublimis in alto,   490

Sub palmâ residens; Sol desuper aureus; *Ecce!*

Evasit! clamat, *felix est ille, canitque*

'*Gloria in excelsis:*' *fulgentem desuper illi*

Justitiæ Solem video, palmasque sacratas,

Unde olim stravere viam gens læta canentum

'*Gloria in excelsis;*' hîc somno excussa, Philippum

Fixa animo arcessit, trepidâque ita voce profatur,

Nil superest quod jam connubia nostra moretur.

Ergo, perque Deum, et per commoda nostra, Philippus,
Nubere si constat, cave ne quid differat horam. 5'?

Conjugio pacto, campanæ læta sonabant ;
Lætitiæ sonitum sparsere per æthera vent'.
Sed nunquam læto exultavit pectore felix
Annia ; cui, quocunque iret, comes additus ibat,
Invisus gradiens ; auditus in aure susurrus,
Nesciit unde cadens ; neque erat contenta relinqui
Sola, domo vacuâ, nec sola exire volebat.
Ecquid erat causæ, quòd vespere sæpe revertens
Ante fores staret, clavemque incerta teneret,
Formidans intrare ? unum se scire Philippus   510
Credidit ; hoc dubios inter fluitare timores
Parturientis erat : sed cum semel editus infans,
Tum novus ille infans vitam renovavit et ipsi,
Tum nova fervebat circum præcordia mater,
Tum complebat ei bonus omnia vota Philippus,
Exoluitque pavor non enarrabilis ille.

Ast Enochus ubi ? læto dedit omine vela

Navigium Fortuna; dies licet haud ita multos

Post abitum Oceani moles Atlantica, fluctus

Præruptos cumulans ad Gallica litora, quassam   520

Pæne ratem obruerit; tanto hoc erepta periclo

Tuta per æstivum mundi translabitur orbem ;

Tum jactata diu circa Caput, omnimodasque

Cœlorum perpessa vices, pelagique dolosi,

Illa, per æstatem rursus transvecta, perennes

Accepit velis gavisa tumentibus auras ;

Thuriferasque inter labens feliciter oras,

Eöo tandem in portu composta quievit.

Illic Enochus commercia propria gessit,

Miraque monstra, domi rursus vendenda, coëmit,   530

Et pueris placiturum auro squamisque draconem.

Sors non tam felix redeunti : primitus autem

Æquora per tranquilla, polo laqueata sereno,

Leni vix nutans libramine, nocte dieque,

FORTUNA intentis oculis, gremioque tumenti,

E prorâ despexit aquas utrinque comantes ;

Tum mare sedatum, et semper variabilis aura ;

Inde dies multos contraria cunêta ; supremùm,

Dum navem abripiunt nigrâ sub noête procellæ,

Per tenebras subito vox est audita pericli   540

Instantis ; fragor horrendus ; funesta ruina ;

Cum binis aliis Enocho sospite.

                    Noêtem

Dimidiam, tabulis sustenti, et fragmine multo,

Hi jaêtantur aquis: quos insula mane recepit,

Dives ea, in solo sed desertissima ponto.

    Illic nulla erat humani penuria viêtûs,

Sponte tulit mites fruêtus uberrima tellus,

Sponte nuces magnas, radices robur alentes ;

Et, sineret pietas, animalia plurima prædam

Perfacilem, feritate ipsâ mansueta, dedissent.   550

Tres ergo e multis silvestri in montis hiatu

Fecerunt caveam, longa æquora prospicientem,

Vivum claudentes foliis palmestribus antrum :

Et sic, frugiferâ in paradiso sorte locati,

Sed male contenti, vixere, æstate perenni.

Unus enim, natu minimus, primâque juventâ,

Naufragio illius noftis subitâque ruinâ

Læsus, tres vitam traxit moribundus in annos ;

Soliciti fovere illum. Post funera, bini

Mœrentes socii truncum invenere jacentem ;   560

Quem, lintrem meditans, dum vitæ prodigus alter

Igne cavat, ritu Indorum, sub sole furenti

Concidit iftus humi : Enochusque, superstes et unus,

Agnovit DOMINUM geminatâ morte monentem.

Montes vestiti silvis ad culmina ; saltus,

Gramineæque viæ, scandentes ardua cæli ;

Plumigerâ insignis cocos gracilenta coronâ ;

Muscarum et volucrum splendentior igne volatus ;

Effulgens late convolvolus, atque columnas

Arboreas cingens sinuosis flexibus, usque   570

Ad maris et terræ confinia; fulgidus ardor,

Quo semper splendet zona hæc latissima mundi;

Hæc illi ante oculos; sed, quod super omnia avebat

Cernere, nusquam aderat facies humana, benigne

Arridens; nec vox audita est dulce loquentis:

Audiit innumeros ululare ad litora mergos;

Immanes fluctus submersa in saxa tonantes;

Perpetuum murmur procera ex arbore, ramis

Floriferis findente polum; lapsumve loquacem

Præcipitis rivi ex alto properantis in æquor;

Litore ut in solo errabat, vel sæpe diebus

Continuis spectabat aquas e montis hiatu;

Naufragus, expectans si posset cernere velum.

Mille dies, bis mille dies, nullum undique velum;

Mille dies, bis mille, orientis spicula Solis

Per palmas rutilant, per fronde comantia saxa;

Fulgor ab Eois radians innubilus undis;

Fulgor ab ætherio descendens acrior axe;

Fulgor ab occiduis radians innubilus undis;

Inde globi astrorum ingentes per concava cœli,

Oceani gravior fremitus; rursusque dici

Spicula surgentis rutilant;—nullum undique velum.

Sæpe ibi dum, similis vigilanti, in sede manebat,

Aurea non timuit coram spe&are lacerta;

Tum spe&ra ante oculos, multis variata figuris,

Injussu fluitare; vel ultro spe&ra ciebat,

Res et personas, quas insula noverat olim,

Orbe alio, ardentique minus sub sole remota;

Infantes balbos, humili sub tegmine matrem,

Scandentem vicum, dominantem turre molinam,

Frondiferos calles, ubi solis stabat in agris

Aula vetus, taxi pavonem imitantis in umbrâ;

Cornipedem socium, lintrem quem totus amavit,

Sub matutino juga frigida rore Novembris,

Stillantes pluvias, silvæ marcentis odorem,

Et circa, marium glaucorum flebile murmur.

Immo, cùm variis tremerent tinnitibus aures,

Audiit, at raptim, pelagi super æquora longe,

E templo veteri campanas læta sonantes;

Tum, quanquam causæ ignarus, formidine tristi

Concitus exsiluit; cùmque insula dives, egena,

In mentem rediit, nisi toto pectore mœrens

Orasset DOMINUM, qui cum simul omnibus adsit,

Fidentes ipsi penitus vetat esse relictos,

Solus ibi vacuas vitam expirasset in auras.

Jam caput Enochi, canescens ocyus æquo,

Pertulerat soles, pluviosaque tempora, longâ

Annorum serie; nec spes diuturna videndi

Dilectos iterum vultus, iterum arva vagandi

Per nota, occiderat, cùm sors ea sola gravisque

Finem habuit subitum. Casu ratis altera, siccis

Pæne cadis, ventoque, velut FORTUNA, frementi

Abrepta, hæc eadem prope litora mansit, ubi esset

Nescia; nauclerusque orienti sole notârat,

(Quà potuit, nebulas per hiantes, insula cerni)

Lympharum tacitos lapsus de collibus; et jam

Oræ cymba subest, nautæ potiuntur arenâ,

Fusîque exultim, quærentes undique rivum,

Vel salientis aquæ fontem, clamoribus implent

Litora. Silvestri gradiens de montis hiatu 630

Descendit, barbâque comans et crinibus Exul

Horridus incomptis, ardenti sole perustus,

Vix specie humanâ, pannoso mirus amictu,

Balba loquens, quasi mentis inops, similisque furenti,

Murmure confuso mussans, nutuque manuque

Signa iterans penitus non intellecta; sed ille

Interea ad loca nota nimis, viridantia rivis,

Duxit, ubi dulces trepidabant in mare lymphæ ;

Dumque ibi se nautis ultro sociabat, eorum

Colloquia auscultans, in vocem et verba soluta est 640

Lingua ligata diu, renovans commercia vitæ ;

Et quæ narravit, fractim licet, ordine nullo,

Credita vix primò, sed mox magis et magis, omnes

Attonitos tristesque simul fecere loquendo.

Jamque, cadis plenis, secum cepere benigni

In navem, vestesque ultro reditumque dedere

In patriam; sed sponte suâ sæpe ille laborem

Participat, vitæ solius vincula gaudens

Excutere. At nemo regione exortus eâdem

Omnibus ex nautis aderat, nec dicere quisquam 650

Enocho poterat, quod primum scire petebat.

Tarda ratis, longæque moræ; compagibus ipsis

Vix secura fides; semper tamen ille morantes

Gaudebat veloci animo prævertere ventos

Festinans; donec dubiæ sub lumine lunæ,

Lætus amator uti, per venas imbibit omnes

Mane novo gelidis stillantes roribus auras,

Litoris Angliaci super ardua mœnia vectas:

Et sole exorto cuncti, nautæque ducesque,

Unanimi pietate sibi imposuere tributum, 660

Soliusque viri miserantes fata dederunt:

Æquore tum placido radentes litora, portu

Enochum exponunt unde olim excesserat ipso.

Illic non verbum fari, non visere quemquam,

Vult—mora nulla, domum—sibi si domus ulla supersit—

Ire pedes properat. Claro Sol pronus in undas

Temperat orbe gelu; donec per chasmata bina,

Quà maris in gremium pandit se portus uterque,

Glaucus ab Oceano volvens tegit omnia nimbus,

Porrectamque viam ante oculos præcludit cunti,   670

Et spatium brevius concedit utrinque, rubeti

Marcentis, prati viridis, vel arabilis agri:

Arbore de nudâ queribunda rubecula luctum

Ingeminat, passimque per aëra rore madentem

Pondere victa suo frons mortua decidit: et jam

Guttatim pluere, et circum densarier umbræ;

Vivida lux demum, sed multâ in nube laborans,

Ante oculos effusa, locum declarat avitum.

Tum lentis pedibus declivi in tramite vici

Descendens, animo prælibans omnia mœsta,   680

Defixis oculis, casulam devenit, ubi olim

Annia conjugio felix adamaverat ipsum,

Et soboles septem nimium felicibus annis

Nata fuit; sed cum sileant sine luce fenestræ,—

(Præconis jam charta fores signaverat)—ultra

Descendit, reputans, *vel mortua, vel mihi saltem.*

Jamque sinum, atque arctâ devenit margine portum,

Hospitium quærens, longinquo a tempore notum;

Frons cujus fuerat tignis contexta vetustis,

Fulta, labansque adeo, lentâque exesa ruinâ,   695

Ut vix speraret superesse; superstite vero

Hospitio, dominus decesserat; et viduata

Martha domum, quæstu semper minuente, tenebat:

Nautis illa frequens olim rixantibus, at nunc

Tranquilla, et fessis requiem præbere parata;

Tristis ibi Enochus longum tacitusque quievit.

Martha autem exundans pietate, et garrula linguæ,

Non solum sinit esse virum; sed sæpe recurrens

Narravit, portûs inter memoranda (quis esset

Nescia, tam capite incurvo, tam sole perustus,   700

Tam miser ille,) domûs fuerint quæ fata relictæ;

Infantis mortem, dum semper egentior uxor;

Miserit ut pueros ad ludum cura Philippi

Nunquam deficiens; ut longum solicitata,

Annia vix votis potuisset cedere; sero

Tandem conjugio junctos, natumque Philippo
Infantem : perque ora viri non transiit umbra,
Nòn tremor insolitus : qui præsens forte fuisset,
Dixisset sentire illum demissa per aures
Narratrice minus : solum cùm clauderet illa,
Enochus, miser ille, abjectâ est nave peremtus,
Ille, caput canum quassans ad tristia verba,
Ingeminat mœrens, *abjectâ nave peremtus ;*
Interiusque gemens iterum imo a corde, *peremtus.*

Ardebat verò dilectum cernere vultum
Enochus ; *si possem iterum semel aspicere illam,*
Si scirem certè felicem vivere. Voti
Impatiens tandem, et stimulo quasi concitus acri,
Exiit ad clivum, cùm lux obscura Novembris
Pallidior fieret, tegerentque crepuscula cœlum :
Illic consedit, contemplans subdita cuncta,
Dum mille angebant vitæ simulacra prioris
Infando mœrore animum. Mox ecce per umbras
Effulsit rutilans geniali luce fenestra,

(Posterior pars illa domûs bene nota Philippi)
Allexitque illum, ceu signifer allicit ignis
Migrantem volucrem, dum fati nescia pennâ
Præcipiti impingat, vitamque extundat anhelam.

Ultima enim vici stabat domus ampla Philippi,
Fronte viam spectans; adversâ ex parte jacebat   730
Hortulus, ad clivum ducens, (unde exitus unus)
Quadratus formâ, muro circumdatus; illic
Taxus perpetuo frondens annosa vigebat;
Semita circuitum cingebat, strata lapillis
Litoreis, mediumque secabat semita septum.
Sed mediam Enochus refugit, furtimque propinquans
Muro subrepit, taxo celatus; et inde
Vidit quæ melius vitasset, si quid in illâ
Fortunâ melius possit pejusve vocari.

Pocula enim in lautâ nituere argentea mensâ,   740
Icta coruscanti circum genialiter igne;

Conspexitque foci dextrâ de parte Philippum,

Non ita felicem quem nôrant tempora prisca,

Robustum, rubicundum, infans cui genua premebat;

Et superimpendens patri post terga secundo,

Serior at formâ procerior Annia, flavis

Crinibus, et vultu stabat speĉtanda ; manuque

Tænia ab elatâ discum vibrabat eburnam,

Infanti illecebras, qui brachia mollia tendens,

Captabat, semper frustra, ridentibus illis.   750

Atque ibi visa foci genitrix de parte sinistrâ,

Quæ repetens oculis infantem sæpe tenellum,

Interdum tamen aspexit, cervice reflexâ,

Astantem lateri juvenili robore natum,

Lætum aliquid memorans, nam risum verba movebant.

Mortuus ut verò redivivus talia vidit,

Uxorem, nec ut ante suam, tenerumque puellum,

Ex illâ genitrice, alio genitore, paternis

In genibus, pacemque foci et felicia cunĉta ;

Progeniemque suam, juvenili robore pulchram,   760

6

Adscitumque illum, regnantem in sede paternâ,
Jure novo in pueros dominantem et amore fruentem ;
Tum quanquam rem Martha priùs narraverat omnem,
Sed quia visa magis mentem quam audita lacessunt,
Contremuit, ramumque tenens vix continuit se,
Quin subito invitus clamorem emitteret acrem,
Qui veluti clangens tuba, mundi fine propinquo,
Lætitiam pacemque foci confringeret omnem.

Ille igitur furtim retro vestigia torquens,
Ne streperet sonitu sibi sub pede glarea duro ;
Contrectansque manu murum, ne forte labaret
Deliquio, inventusque jacens se proderet illis ;
Ad portam repens, aperit, clauditque, cavendo
Solicite, ægroti cameram ceu claudit amicus ;
Exitque in clivum, cœli sub tegmine solus.
Tum si non infirma nimis sibi genua labâssent,
Orâsset supplex ; sed labens pronus in udam
Figit humum digitos, imoque ex corde precatur ;

Dura nimis! cur me exilio rapuistis ab illo?
O DEUS omnipotens, Salvator Maxime, qui me 780
Fovisti, solo ducentem in litore vitam;
Amplius O tueare, Pater, nam solus in orbe,
Solus adhuc vivo: adsistas mihi, des mihi vires,
Ne vocem emittam, ne me sciat illa reversum;
Auxiliare, domûs ne pacem abrumpere cogar.
At mea progenies! nec compellare licebit
Ignaros qui sim? ipse mei sed proditor essem;
Oscula nulla mihi, cùm sim pater—hei mihi, matri
Filia tam similis, genitori filius ille.

Tum voce, atque animo paullum defecit; humique 790
Deliquium passus jacuit; tandemque resurgens
Ille domum versus repetens vestigia solam
Ibat descendens angusto tramite vici,
Ingeminans lasso tristissima verba cerebro,
Ceu decantato redeuntem in carmine versum,
Ne vocem emittam, ne me sciat illa reversum.

Non erat omnino infelix ; duravit in illo
Firma fides, animusque tenax ; semperque perenni
Fonte preces sursum salientes pectore ab imo,
Urgentesque viam per amari flumina luctus,
Ceu lymphæ dulces salientes æquore salso,
Vitalem fovere animam : *Sed nupta Philippi*
Quam mihi commemoras, Martham sic ille rogavit,
Nonne timet ne vivat adhuc prior ille maritus ?

Me miseram ! *timet illa nimis,* pia femina clamat ;
Si posses illum testari morte peremtum,
Non leve solamen dederis ; sibi murmurat ille,
Postquam me Dominus dimiserit, omnia noscet,
Expectanda dies. Operam tum suscipit ultro,
Unde alimenta paret, spernens ex munere vitam ;
Artibus ille manum variis aptaverat usu ;
Dolia compingit, tractat fabrilia ; noctu
Retia contexit, genti metuenda marinæ ;
Sæpe rates celsas onerando, aut exonerando,
Quæ sæcli illius commercia parva ferebant,)
Auxilium præbens, tenuem sibi comparat escam :

At pro se solo, nec spe fallente laborem,

Impendebat opus, neque erant solatia in illo,

Unde aleret vitam; et cùm se revolubilis annus

Verteret, atque diem jam brumâ ineunte referret

Enochi memorem reditûs, tum languidus illum

Oppressit torpor, tabes lentissima, vires

Absumens, tandemque operi decedere cogens;

Intusque affixit sellæ, demumque cubili.

Sed forti Enochus toleravit pectore morbum;

Nam certè, nave abjectâ, non lætior unquam

Apparet, glauci per hiantia fragmina nimbi,

Jam desperatis inopinam ferre salutem

Linter festinans, quam tunc apparuit illi

Exoriens lethi facies, finisque malorum.

Hoc etenim augurio exoritur spes lætior illi,

Dicenti secum, *cùm vita reliquerit artus,*

Tum discet conjux, me ad finem semper amâsse;

Martham ergo appellans elatâ voce profatur;

Arcanum servo, mulier—sed in hoc mihi jura—

Non prius edicam—Libro dans oscula jura,

Te nihil ante foras—quàm mortuus ipse quiescam.

Mortuus, exclamat bona femina, *qualia fatur!*

Crede mihi, amissas vires reparare licebit.

Enochus graviter, *Libro dans oscula, jura.*

Et tacto exanimis juravit femina libro.

Cæsia tum volvens Enochus lumina in illam,

Nôrasne Enochum, genitor cui naufragus, Arden?

Illum ego num nossem? longinquo a tempore nôram:

Immo etiam memini, ut vicum descenderet olim,

Elato capite, haud quenquam respexerit ille.

Enochus lentâ suspirans voce reponit ;

Nunc humili capite est, nec quisquam respicit illum:

Vix mihi quatriduum durabit spiritus ; audi,

Ille ego sum. Audito mulier dedit excita vocem,

Ceu non credibili mentem pessundata verbo :

Tune ille Enochus? quis crederet! altior ille

Te multò fuit ille: Enochus tristior addit,

Me DEUS *incurvum fecit, qualem aspicis esse;*

Me fregit dolor, et solius tædia vitæ;

47

Ne verò dubites, ego sum qui tempore prisco

Duxi—sed quam te memorem, bis nomine verso?—

Illa fuit conjux mea, quæ nunc nupta Philippo est;

Asside, et ausculta. Tum cuncta ex ordine narrat,

Naufragium, exiliique moras, reditûsque dolorem ;   860

Ut furtim uxorem conspexerit, ut sibi legem

Impositam servârit adhuc : dumque audiit illa,

Manavit facili lacrimarum copia rivo,

Dum corde impatiens arcani femina tanti

Ardebat totum circa discurrere portum,

Enochi reditum vulgans, et tristia fata ;

Sed perculsa metu, pactoque astricta quievit :

Mox *pueros primùm videas* ait illa *necesse est;*

Eia! sine accersam, surgitque ut deferat illos,

Hæsit enim Enochus paullùm ; sed protinus instat ;   870

Ne me turbâris, mulier, jam fine propinquo,

Sed sine propositum suprema ad funera servem.

Assideas iterum, et teneas quæ dicere pergo,

Dum mihi vox superest. Te nunc impensiùs oro,

Cum venias coram, dicas, bona cuncta precantem

Me vitæ ad finem coluisse fideliter illam ;

Me pariter, si non fatum prohiberet, amâsse,

Ac quando mecum vinclo fuit una jugali.

Et natæ, mea quam viderunt lumina, matri

Tam similem, referas, ut spiritus ultimus oris 8.40

Illi exoptando felicia cuncta meârit ;

Et nato tradas moribundi vota parentis,

Sorte, precor, patrem superet ; dicasque Philippo,

Illum etiam partem votorum habuisse meorum ;

Ille nihil nisi quod nobis prodesset avebat.

Quod si me pueri cupiant post fata videre,

Qui me vix nôrant viventem, nil moror illos,

Fas genitorem adeant ; modo ne quis deferat illam,

Mortua nam facies venientes angeret annos.

Unus restat adhuc—unus de sanguine nostro 850

Qui me complexu vitâ recreabit in illâ ;

En ! hunc cincinnum, abscissum de fronte puelli,

Illa dedit ; mecumque tuli tot sedulus annos,

Et mihi mens fuerat vel ad ipsum ferre sepulcrum ;

Sed nunc consilium mutavi; illum ipse beatos
Inter conspiciam: cùm vita recesserit ergo,
Hunc matri tradas; spero, hic solabitur illam,
Saltem erit indicio, quo certe agnoscere possit,
Hunc esse Enochum.

    Dixit; promtissima Martha
Respondit, nimiâque volubilis omnia linguâ
Præstitit; ille autem morientia lumina volvens
Solicite mandata iterat, rursusque rogatam
Martha fidem præstat.

    Sed cùm nox tertia venit,—
Dum jacet in lecto pallens, immobilis, ille,
Dum vigilat mulier bona, dormitatque vicissim,—
Infremuit subitò taii cum turbine surgens
Pontus, ut angusti streperent tecta omnia portûs;
Audiit—exsiluit—jactavit brachia late,
Exclamans voce altisonâ, *velum! aspice! velum!*
Salvus sum! salvus! reciditque haud plura locutus.

Sic anima invictâ pollens virtute recessit ;
Cùm verò efferrent funus, vix lautior unquam
Portum per tenuem deducta est pompa sepulcri.

CANTABRIGIÆ
TYPIS ACADEMICIS EXCUDEBAT C. J. CLAY, A.M

GENEVIEVE.

GENOVEVA.

GENEVIEVE.

ALL thoughts, all wishes, all delights,
Whatever stirs this mortal frame:
All are but ministers of Love,
    And feed his sacred flame.

GENOVEVA.

IMPULSUS animorum omnes, et gaudia vitæ,
  Quicquid mortalem temperiem stimulat ;
Omnia certatim dio famulantur Amori,
  Et flammam accensi cælitus ignis alunt.

Oft in my waking dreams do I
Live o'er again that happy hour,
When midway on the mount I lay,
　Beside the ruined tower.

The moonshine, stealing o'er the scene,
Had blended with the lights of eve;
And she was there, my hope, my joy,
　My own bright Genevieve.

She leant against the armed man,
The statue of the armed knight;
She stood and listened to my lay
　Amid the lingering light.

Few sorrows hath she of her own,
My hope! my joy! my Genevieve!
She loves me best whene'er I sing
　The songs that make her grieve.

Sæpe ego, dum vigiles oblectant somnia sensus,
 Vivo iterum vitæ quæ fuit hora meæ
Felix ante omnes ; ubi turris propter avitæ
 Relliquias medio in colle reclinis eram.

Luna, per æthereas labens argentea nubes,
 Sublustri lucem vespere mista dabat ;
Atque ibi, lux melior, vitæ spes unica nostræ,
 Lætitiæ saliens fons, Genoveva, fuit.

Stabat ibi acclinis statuæ dilecta vetustæ,
 Effusâ attingens militis arma comâ ;
Stabat ibi auscultans, mea dum sub luce moranti
 Fundebat citharâ vox comitante melos.

Perpaucas fovet illa suo sub pectore curas,
 Lætitiæ saliens fons, Genoveva, meæ ;
Nescio cur illi placeam magis, ista canendo
 Carmina quæ tenero corda dolore movent.

I played a soft and doleful air,
I sang an old and moving story;
An old rude song, that suited well
    That ruin wild and hoary.

She listened with a flitting blush,
With downcast eyes, and modest grace;
For well she knew I could not choose,
    But gaze upon her face.

I told her of the Knight that wore
Upon his shield a burning brand;
And that for ten long years he wooed
    The Lady of the Land.

I told her how he pined; and ah!
The deep, the low, the pleading tone,
With which I sang another's love,
    Interpreted my own.

GENOVEVA.

Tangebam lente chordas modulamine mæsto,
 Fabula cui tristis consociata fuit ;
Fabula quæ, veteri tantùm germana ruinæ,
 Ex ipso poterat nata fuisse loco.

Auscultat, volitante vago super ora rubore,
 Ingenuos oculos fixa decenter humi ;
Sensit enim nullo moderamine posse teneri
 Quin faciem haurirent lumina nostra suam.

Narravi quantus Miles viguisset in armis,
 Cui clipei signum flammea tæda fuit ;
Qui prece perpetuâ decimum exoptavit in annum
 Terrarum dominam quas maris unda lavat.

Narravi ut longo absumtus langueret amore,
 Voce meâ teneras restituente preces ;
Dum sic alterius suspiria mæsta canebam,
 Interpres nostri carmen amoris erat.

GENEVIEVE.

She listen'd with a flitting blush,
With downcast eyes and modest grace;
And she forgave me, that I gazed
   Too fondly on her face.

But when I told the cruel scorn,
That crazed that bold and lovely Knight;
And that he crossed the mountain-woods,
   Nor rested day nor night:

That sometimes from the savage den,
And sometimes from the darksome shade;
And sometimes starting up at once
   In green and sunny glade;

There came and looked him in the face
An angel beautiful and bright:
And that he knew it was a fiend,
   This miserable Knight.

Auscultat, volitante vago super ora rubore;
  Ingenuos oculos fixa decenter humi;
Ignovitque mihi, nimio quòd amantia tractu
  Haurirent faciem lumina nostra suam.

Ut vero cecini crudelem virginis iram,
  Qua cecidit magni mens labefacta viri;
Ut montes nemorumque vagus percurreret umbras,
  Nec requiem misero noxve diesve daret;

Ut nunc horrenti egrediens in aperta cavernâ,
  Nunc ubi celaret densior umbra diem;
Et nunc prosiliens, velut herbâ nata virenti,
  Qua daret apricum silva reducta locum;

Obvia se prodens coram spectaret imago,
  Cælicolum referens ora comasque decus:
Ille tamen sciret quam noxia luderet umbra;
  Hic miseri summus terror amantis erat.

And that unknowing what he did,
He leapt amid a murderous band,
And saved from outrage worse than death
   The Lady of the Land.

And how she wept, and clasped his knees,
And how she tended him in vain ;
And ever strove to expiate
   The scorn that crazed his brain.

And that she nursed him in a cave,
And how his madness went away ;
When on the yellow forest-leaves
   A dying man he lay.

His dying words—but when I reach'd
That tenderest strain of all the ditty ;
My faultering voice and pausing harp
   Disturbed her soul with pity.

Prodigus ut vitæ, nullo comitante, ferocem
    Irruerit, facti nescius ipse, manum :
Damno erepturus, quod morte indignius ipsâ,
    Terrarum dominam quas maris unda lavat.

Ut flerit virgo, genibusque pependerit ægris,
    Et frustra advigilans nocte dieque toro
Tentarit semper sævum placare dolorem,
    Quo fuerat magni mens labefacta viri :

Ut pietate fovens ægrum curarit in antro,
    Deficeret victus dum ratione furor ;
Ut foliis stratus marcentibus ille jaceret,
    Marcidior foliis, et moribundus, humi.

Ut verò ventum est morientis ad ultima verba,
    Quo nihil in toto carmine flebilius ;
Vox mea deficiens citharæque silentia mæsta
    Turbarunt dominam religione meam.

All impulses of soul and sense
Had thrilled my guileless Genevieve;
The music and the doleful tale,
   The rich and balmy eve;

And hopes, and fears that kindle hope,
An undistinguishable throng :
And gentle wishes long subdued,
   Subdued, and cherished long.

She wept with pity and delight,
She blushed with love and virgin-shame;
And like the murmur of a dream,
   I heard her breathe my name.

Her bosom heaved; she stept aside,
As conscious of my look she stept :
Then suddenly, with timorous eye,
   She fled to me, and wept.

Omnia quæ tangunt sensus, animumque, movebant
    Imitus expertem te, Genoveva, doli;
Et citharæ melos, et nimiùm lacrimabile carmen,
    Plenaque deliciis vesperis hora suis.

Et spes, spemque novam soliti stimulare timores,
    Turba frequens, nullo dissocianda modo:
Et frænata diu necdum sopita voluntas,
    Dum reprimit motus corde fovente suos.

Lætitiâ in lacrimas simul et pietate soluta est;
    Dulcis amor rubuit, virgineusque pudor;
Et velut auditum dubie per somnia murmur,
    Audivi nomen, contremuique, meum.

Intumuere sinus; paullum conversa retraxit,
    Conscia quid facerent lumina nostra, pedem;
Sed rediens subito, timidoque imbellis ocello,
    Ad mea confugiens pectora flevit ibi.

She half enclosed me with her arms,
She prest me with a meek embrace ;
And bending back her head, looked up,
    And gazed upon my face.

'Twas partly Love, and partly Fear,
And partly 'twas a bashful art,
That I might rather feel than see
    The swelling of her heart.

I calmed her fears, and she was calm ;
And told her love with virgin-pride ;
And so I won my Genevieve,
    My bright and beauteous Bride.

Et diducta meo circumdans brachia collo,
  Amplexu pressit me tenuitque diu ;
Mox rediere animi, et leviter cervice reflexâ
  Hauserunt faciem lumina læta meam.

Partim suasit amor, partim timor æmulus egit,
  Et partim ingenui forma pudoris erat ;
Scilicet ut sentire magis quam cernere possem,
  Quo niveum quaterent corda tremore sinum.

Composui fluctus animi ; tranquilla quievit ;
  Virgineumque loquens se patefecit amor ;
Sic, cithará victor, candentem flore juventæ
  Accepi sponsam te, Genoveva, meam.

W. E. G.

PALINODIA.

In medio gradiens mortalis tramite vitæ,
  Hic ubi celabat densior umbra diem;
Erravi, tenuitque diu me devius error,
  Incertos cogens ferre, referre, pedes;
Vox subito audita est, quæ me revocavit ab umbris,
  Dura quidem auditu vox, sed amica mihi;
Tum Luna auxilio, tingens argentea nubes,
  Fimbria ceu pullæ candida vestis, erat;
Agnovi errorem, et retro vestigia torquens
  Amissam inveni lætus ovansque viam;
Et vidi Templum, cui scriptum in limine prostat,
  ERROREM FASSOS PVLCRA CORONA MANET.

IN DOMO PROCERVM. JVL. 3, A.D. 1871. 5.15 P.M.

CANONICVS MVLTA GEMENS.

SI neque COMMVNES, PROCERESVE in prælia prostant,
    Restitui ut cogant jura negata mihi;
Quid misero restat?—multum plorante crumená,
    REGINÆ ad BANCVM lis referenda mihi est:
Concilii Præses validum MANDAMVS habeto,
    Quod fieri debet protinus ut faciat.
Mens etenim stat fixa animo, defendere LEGES,
    Nec sinere antiquum corruere IMPERIVM.

IN CVRIA BANC. REG.   JAN. 18, A.D. 1872.

PER BLACKBURN, J.

Si Populus, Proceres, Regina, in lege ferendâ
Unanimes fierent—sit procul ille dies—
Ut me damnarent, decollarentque repente,
Lex ea—me saltem judice—firma foret.

REGINÆ CONSILIARIVS.

Causidicos inter, mihi credas, optime Judex,
Lege super tali nulla querela foret.

A.D. 1869 . 1871.

Cvm triplices legum muros perrumperet audax
Lælapis, Hibernas et spoliaret opes:
Nec vocem emisit, sociosve vocavit in arma,
Nec Summus Judex, causidicusve minor.
Ut vero legem Vir Carbonarius unam
Transilit, extemplo perstrepit omne forum.

W. S.
CANTABRIGIÆ.